Books by Fay Cunningham
in the Linford Romance Library:

SNOWBOUND
DECEPTION
LOVE OR MARRIAGE
DREAMING OF LOVE
FORGOTTEN
CHRISTMAS TREES AND MISTLETOE

THE MOONSTONES TRILOGY:
THE RUBY
THE SAPPHIRE
THE EMERALD

KU-483-962

AFTER THE STORM

When Sara loses her job and is turned out of her London flat, she knows her aunt will give her and her young son Jake a temporary home. But on the drive to Norfolk, she takes a wrong turn and gets lost in a violent storm. Desperate to find shelter for the night, they are forced to take refuge in a cabin on a lake. Staying in the cabin next door is handsome Theo Winter, who offers to help Sara — but he has secrets of his own . . .

WITHDRAWN FROM STOCK

FAY CUNNINGHAM

AFTER THE STORM

Complete and Unabridged

LINFORD
Leicester

First published in Great Britain in 2017

First Linford Edition
published 2018

Copyright © 2017 by Fay Cunningham
All rights reserved

A catalogue record for this book is available
from the British Library.

ISBN 978–1–4448–3651–6

Published by
F. A. Thorpe (Publishing)
Anstey, Leicestershire

Set by Words & Graphics Ltd.
Anstey, Leicestershire
Printed and bound in Great Britain by
T. J. International Ltd., Padstow, Cornwall

This book is printed on acid-free paper

1

Sara nearly missed the sign because she wasn't looking for it. She was looking for lights or houses. Any signs of civilisation. Taking the back roads had seemed a good idea at the time, but now she was so tired she was worried she might fall asleep at the wheel. It was almost ten o'clock, and she had to find somewhere to spend the night. Somewhere safe.

The reason she hadn't seen the sign was because it was partly obscured by the waving branches of a tree. There one minute, gone the next, like an optical illusion. After a quick look behind, her she slowed, pulling up tight against the side of the road. DANTE'S LAKE, the sign said. CABINS FOR RENT.

She turned round to look at the seat behind her, and then risked putting on the interior light so she could look at her map. Where on earth was Dante's Lake? Nowhere on her map, that was for sure. She turned off the light and peered at the sign again. It was raining, and the wind had increased almost to a gale, forcing the trees to bend under its attack. Stuck in the middle of nowhere in a storm wasn't where Sara wanted to be. Deciding she hadn't got much choice, she turned down what was barely more than a cart track, ducking when a gust of wind whipped a branch across her windscreen. Any port in a storm, she thought, as she drove down the narrow lane.

Slowly, slowly ... anything more than walking pace would have been lethal. She set her lights on dip, concentrating on staying in the ruts already carved out in front of her. She had no idea where she was heading and, after a couple of minutes with no sign of a lake or a cabin, she began to wonder if she had made a horrible mistake. But there was nowhere to turn around, and in this sort of weather any sort of manoeuvring would have been lethal. After rounding a corner she almost failed to negotiate, she saw the lights of a house: a golden glow shining through the driving rain like a friendly beacon.

Turning onto a parking area in front of the house, she pulled up as close as she could to the front door and sat for a moment, half-hoping someone might come out with an umbrella to greet her, but no such luck. She couldn't blame them. The wind was shaking the trees overhead and driving the rain in random gusts against the car so hard it sounded like hail.

The house was a two-storey brick-built box with a set of windows on either side of the front door. That was about all she could see in the dark. There was a solitary car parked off to one side, a light in one of the downstairs windows, and a light over the door, so presumably someone was still up. Still no sign of any cabins, though.

With another worried glance at the seat beside her, she pushed the car door open and hopped quickly outside. The wind almost wrenched the door out of her hand, but she managed to shut it and run the few yards to the house, where a glass door led into a small porch-like area. The door opened easily and she slipped inside out of the rain. In front of her was another door, presumably leading into the house; a heavy wooden affair with a stained-glass panel at the top. Her hair was clinging to her face and her thin jacket was already soaked, but mercifully the door opened almost as soon as she rang the bell.

A pleasant-faced woman with fluffy fair hair looked out at her. 'I thought I heard a car. Oh, you poor thing, you're soaked. Please come inside.'

Sara stood her ground. 'Thank you, but I'd rather not come in. I'll drip all over your floor. My name is Sara Finch. The sign said cabins for rent. Do you have any vacancies?'

'If you come inside for a moment . . . '

'I'm fine. Really.'

The woman gave her a curious glance but called over her shoulder to someone inside, 'Gareth, which cabin is vacant?'

A boy of about fourteen or fifteen appeared at the bottom of a long narrow hallway and walked towards them. 'Cabin three is empty, Mum.' He looked at Sara. 'You're a bit wet.'

'I think I must have taken a wrong turn, but I don't think it's safe to drive any further in this storm. I need somewhere to spend the night.'

'We won't ask you to sign anything until tomorrow. You need to get out of those wet clothes. Besides, you don't look the kind of person to run off with the furniture.' She reached up to a hook on the wall and took down a key with a plastic tab attached. 'Cabin three. There are only five cabins, so three is right in the middle — you can't miss it — and the parking is at the side, under cover.' She handed Sara the key. 'I'll send Gareth down in the morning and get you to sign in. If you can hang on a minute, I'll fix you up a box of staples, milk and things, to keep you going until the morning. We always put a box in the cabin for a new guest.'

'Thank you,' Sara said politely. 'But I have groceries in the car.' She was still standing in the lobby and could see her car through the glass door, but she needed to get back.

'I'm Felicity Cartwright,' the woman said, 'and this is my son, Gareth. I keep the heating on low in the empty cabins, and there will be lights and hot water. You can turn the heating up if you feel cold. It's supposed to be spring, almost summer now, but it doesn't feel like it.' She gave Sara a sympathetic look. 'Get in the warm before you catch a chill.'

'Thank you,' Sara said again, hurrying outside before the woman could delay her any longer. She closed the outside door and ran the few yards to her car. She could see the woman and her son still watching as she slipped into the driver's seat.

The storm had picked up its pace while she was inside. It was noisy now, whistling through the trees and sending bushes dancing like dervishes along the narrow lane. She had only gone a few yards, her headlights on full beam, when a branch crashed down in front of her. Somehow she managed to avoid it without going into the ditch, and at that moment a clearing opened up ahead. She could see a glint of water under the black sky. Presumably Dante's Lake.

Quietly cursing the circumstances that had brought her here, she inched the car forwards. She was used to well-paved roads and street lights; someone to ask directions if you got lost and a garage just round the corner if you broke down.

Behind her Jake grunted and she shushed him automatically. *Sleep a little longer*, she silently begged, *at least until she found the cabin*. She knew how grumpy he could be if he got woken up before he was ready.

The cabins were laid out in a crescent around the shallow curve of the lake. Five long, low wooden rectangles built on stilts, with a raised wooden deck running along the front of each and a covered parking space to the side. There was a coach lantern outside each cabin, three of them turned on. She bumped over long wet grass and parked on the flat area beside the middle cabin. Open both ends, the car-port gave little cover in this sort of weather, but at least it would keep some of the rain off while she unpacked what she needed for the night. There were wooden steps up to the door of the cabin but they were round the front, out in the open. She turned off the ignition, trying to work out what to take in first. She didn't want to make too many journeys in the rain, but she didn't want to leave Jake by himself in case he woke up.

A knock on the car window right beside her almost gave her heart failure. She jumped violently, her heart beating a frantic tattoo inside her chest. The first thing she saw was a man's face peering at her through the glass. Her brain was telling her to scream, but her throat had closed and all she could manage was a little squeak. He knocked again, a gentle tap this time. He must have seen how much he'd startled her. When she saw his umbrella, logic pushed her heart rate back down to almost normal and she opened the window a crack. She thought for a moment it might be Gareth, come to see if she had reached the cabin safely. But the owner of the umbrella had short dark hair and matching stubble on his chin.

'Sorry I made you jump.' He bent down to peer at her through the narrow gap she had made. 'I have an umbrella.'

She had already noticed that, it was difficult to miss when it kept trying to turn inside out, so she kept quiet, hoping his voice wouldn't wake Jake. She couldn't get a good look at his face because he was wearing a jacket with the hood pulled up, but he had a nice voice. When she still didn't say anything, he shrugged.

'I'll either help you get your things out of the car, or I'll go back to my cabin and you can get wet on your own. Your choice. My name is Theo, and I'm renting the cabin next door.' A sudden gust of wind dislodged his hood and he pulled it back up again. 'I'm sure I look pretty scary at the moment, but that's the fault of the storm. Normally I'm quite a nice, ordinary guy.'

She smiled, even though she tried not to, and opened the car door. She handed him the cabin key. 'Thank you. If you could go round the front of the cabin and unlock the door for me, that would be a great help.'

He was back in seconds. 'I put the door on the latch but it keeps blowing open. Look, let's get you inside out of the rain, and then you can tell me what you need brought in from the car.'

'That won't work,' she said.

He followed her gaze to the back seat. 'Yes it will. I'll carry him in first. How old is he?'

'Four. He gets really grumpy if he wakes up suddenly.'

'Then I won't wake him. I have a nephew about his age. You take the umbrella and I'll get your son inside as quickly as possible.'

She couldn't see how that was going to work, either; Jake was quite tall for his age. But somehow it did. Theo undid the seat belt and swept Jake up into his arms. Within seconds they were all inside the cabin, the child grumbling but miraculously still asleep. He must have been exhausted, poor lamb.

She looked round the room and pointed to a large comfy-looking sofa. 'Put him down there. I'll bring the rest of the stuff in when he wakes.'

Now they were inside, and he'd pushed off his hood, she could get a better look at her rescuer. A couple of inches over six feet, she decided, but broad as well as tall. A lot of it muscle,

11

judging from the way he'd picked up Jake. The dark stubble was quite attractive and the slight cleft in his chin was interesting. She watched as he laid Jake gently down on the sofa.

'He looks as if he's crashed out till morning. What do you need from the car?'

Sara looked at her rescuer and sighed. She wasn't going to get rid of him easily. 'A suitcase from the boot and the shopping bag from the back seat. And the car needs to be locked up again. You don't have to do this, you know. I can manage fine on my own.'

He held out his hand for her car keys. 'I'm sure you can. But right now you're not on your own, and I'd hate to have got myself this wet for nothing.' He was back in minutes and gave her back her keys. 'One suitcase and a bag of groceries? Is that all you have with you?'

'I didn't plan on stopping off anywhere, but then the weather got too bad to carry on.' She knew that didn't answer his question, but it would have to do for the time being. 'We have clothes and food. I also have coffee and tea, and some milk, so I can make us a drink.' She looked at the man called Theo who appeared to be as wet as she was. 'You probably need a hot drink as much as I do. Can I make you a cup of tea?'

She saw him hesitate, but then he nodded. 'Thank you.'

She didn't know why she was doing this. She didn't know anything about the man, and she should know better than to ask a stranger into her cabin. But right this moment, she was just grateful for his help.

She took his wet jacket and hung it over the back of a dining chair, then walked into the tiny kitchenette and filled the electric kettle at the sink. Up until that point she hadn't had time to check her surroundings. The living area took up most of the cabin, narrowing at the bottom into a smaller space with a dining table and two chairs. The kitchen was part of the dining area, little more than a counter top with a small sink and a hob with an oven underneath. Sufficient, she thought, for all the cooking she intended to do.

With the kettle humming on the worktop, she opened the other two doors and looked inside. A large bedroom with two single beds behind one door, a bathroom with a shower cubicle, washbasin and toilet behind the other. Having Jake in the same room with her was fine, he would need her close for a few days, but he liked to have a bath before she tucked him up for the night, so the shower could be a problem. Too bad, she thought; they were both going to have to make sacrifices. She was just wondering why she couldn't contact her aunt, and how long they could stay in the cabin before they ran out of money, when the kettle came to the boil and switched itself off.

She had almost forgotten Theo, but when she turned round he was watching her with keen slate-grey eyes.

'The cabins aren't bad. Plenty of hot water and electricity. You'll have to share a bedroom with the boy, though. Will that be a problem?'

Sara shook her head. 'No, we're used to it.' She would have to be careful, she realised. She didn't like answering questions. Questions had a habit of tripping you up. 'We lived in a one-bedroom flat for a while.'

He took the mug she handed him and drank his tea in silence. Rather than sit next to him, she sat opposite on a chair that matched the sofa. Theo was an unassuming name, she thought, but the man drinking tea so hot it should have burned the roof of his mouth didn't look at all unassuming. For one thing, he was older than she had first thought. Probably in his early thirties, maybe even older. His face was tanned, but the red marks on his cheekbones made her think he wasn't used to much sun on his face.

The damp polo shirt clinging to his chest showed ridges of muscle that only came from working out, or a very strenuous job, and the long fingers curling round his mug looked strong enough to strangle someone. She'd been stupid to invite the man in without knowing anything about him. But then she had a long history of doing stupid things. There were a number of people who would testify to that.

She got up from her chair when Jake stirred in his sleep. 'I should get him to bed.'

'Yes, of course. Thanks for the tea.' He got as far as the door and then put his hand in the pocket of his jeans and pulled out a slim wallet. He handed her a business card. 'My mobile number is on there. If you need anything, I'm only next door.'

He let himself out, pulling the door shut against the wind. She heard him give it a bang from outside to make sure it was closed securely.

Sara looked at the card he had given her. His name was at the top. Theodore Winter. There were some letters after his name, and then two phone numbers; one a mobile number and the other presumably his home phone. She turned the card over, but the other side was blank. Usually there was the name of a company, or a more detailed job description on a business card, and she didn't recognise the groups of letters. He could be anything from a doctor to a plumber, and Theo Winter didn't look like either. She shrugged and bent to kiss her sleeping son on the forehead. Then she went into the bedroom to unpack their few belongings.

She turned down one of the twin beds, ready for Jake if he woke up. If not, she would carry him in and take off his jacket and shoes. She'd done that before without waking him, and he was quite happy to sleep in his clothes. What had happened to their lives? she wondered. Not long ago, Jake had been happy in his day nursery and she had a

17

good job. Their flat wasn't very big but, for London the rent had been reasonable. All in all, things had been pretty good.

Now they were homeless.

2

Jake woke in the night and for a moment Sara was disoriented, unable to remember where she was. She managed to take him to the toilet and get him out of his clothes and into his pyjamas without properly waking him. He grunted crossly a few times, but he was so tired he went back to sleep almost immediately. Sleep didn't come so easily to Sara. She was used to the noise of traffic, and here there was a silence so complete it had a sound of its own.

After half an hour of tossing and turning, she got up and went into the tiny kitchen. With the bedroom door closed, she was able to turn on the small light over the hob and make herself another cup of tea. She had packed cocoa somewhere because Jake liked it, but now was not the time to start hunting for it, and anyway she was too tired to bother. Tea would have to do.

The storm had blown itself out sometime during the early part of the night, so she risked opening the sliding glass door onto the deck. The lake looked like black glass, a strip of moonlight cutting across the surface like a liquid pathway. Something made the water ripple. A fish, or maybe an otter, as silent as the night, the only evidence a whisper of shingle moving at the water's edge. The sky looked lighter in the east and she looked at her watch. Almost daylight. Time she got some more sleep before Jake started asking for his breakfast. She was about to go back inside when a small sound caught her attention. The cabin next to hers was dark, but someone was sliding open the door onto the deck.

She moved back inside her doorway, but Theo Winter's cabin was at a slight angle to hers so she saw him step outside. He moved quietly, a shadowy ghost wearing boxer shorts and not much else. Fascinated, she watched him walk to the rail overlooking the lake. He glanced across at her cabin, but she doubted he could see her. She kept very still as she watched him rest his arms on the rail and stare out over the water. Someone else who couldn't sleep. She wondered what was keeping Mr Winter awake.

If she moved now, he was bound to notice her and it would look as if she was spying on him, so she stayed where she was, and after a few minutes he went back inside. She waited a bit longer before she moved, in case he was watching her cabin, which was probably paranoid; but over the last few months she had convinced herself paranoia was a good survival tactic.

She climbed back into bed and, in spite of the fact that she had been sure she would stay awake until morning, fell asleep almost immediately. She awoke with a start, and almost a scream, when Jake whispered in her ear.

'Mummy, is it morning? I'm hungry.'

Sara could vaguely remember a time when her only worry in the morning was Jake's breakfast, but it seemed like a long time ago. 'I have to find the cereal,' she told him as she pulled on her jeans. 'And you need a wash. Let's get you all nice and clean and then you can choose what you want to eat.'

The lack of a bath was just another obstacle to overcome. Jake didn't like having a shower. He didn't like the water falling on his head, so once she had the water at the right temperature, she allowed Jake to hold the shower head and soak himself all over while she sponged him down. Necessity was the mother of invention, and she was fast learning to be particularly inventive.

'Do you know where we are?' she asked as she patted him dry. 'You were asleep when we got here last night.'

'Was there a man? I think a man carried me.'

'Yes. He carried you into the cabin. He's staying next door to us.' Sara found some clothes that didn't look too rumpled, reminding herself to ask about an iron, and helped Jake dress himself. Over the last year he had become fiercely independent. 'Come and see where we are, Jake. There's a lake right outside. A lake is like a big pond.'

Jake took her hand. 'Does it have fish in it?'

'I have no idea,' Sara said as she pulled back the curtains. 'But it's certainly big enough.'

'Wow!' Jake was already pulling on the door handle, too impatient to wait while she unlocked the door. He ran out onto the deck, oblivious to the early morning chill. 'I can see a boat. Can we go for a boat ride?'

Sara followed his pointing finger. The lake was hazy with an early morning mist but she spotted the boat, a little wooden dingy pulled up on the shoreline near the first cabin.

'I'll find out, but let's get you that breakfast first.'

'There's a man over there.'

Jake was pointing in the opposite direction this time, and Sara had to peer into the mist to see anything at all. But Jake was right. A man was walking down the path that skirted the lake. He wasn't exactly running, but he was walking fast towards the cabins, a small dog skipping at his feet. As he got nearer she recognised him. Theo Winter. With a dog this time, and a definite limp. She hadn't remembered him limping the night before, but then she hadn't really been looking.

As he got nearer, he waved a hand and slowed down. There was very little sign that he favoured his right leg, and you might never know unless you had seen him doing what amounted to a power walk. She wondered if he had been right round the lake.

The little dog bounced up to the deck rail and stood on its hind legs, its front feet between the bars of the wooden rail. It had a tail like a pump handle that was wagging so furiously the whole of the dog's body shook. Sara bent down to scratch the blunt head.

'A staffy,' she said with a smile. 'A Staffordshire Bull Terrier. My granddad had one.'

Theo Winter leant forward from the waist to rest his hands on his knees. 'She's my sister's dog. The family have gone to Disneyland, so she's keeping me company.'

He didn't sound out of breath, and he should have been after walking that fast. Particularly with a bad leg. Sara laughed when her head-scratching became too much for the dog and it rolled on its back in ecstasy.

Jake dropped to his knees and peered through the bars. 'What's her name?'

'Rosie.' Winter looked at Sara and grinned. 'Not my idea. My sister has no sense of suitability.'

Jake glanced at his mother. 'Can I go down the steps and pet her?'

'If Mr Winter says it's OK. Mind how you go.' She watched him carefully manoeuvre the wooden steps and go round to the front of the cabin. He looked at Theo Winter for permission before touching the dog.

'Go ahead. She'll take as much petting as she can get.' He smiled up at Sara. 'Can you both call me Theo, please?'

Sara felt herself blush, something she hadn't done for a long time. What was there about this man that unsettled her? He was wearing shorts today. Long shorts that stopped just past his knees, trainers without socks on his feet, and a sleeveless vest marked with patches of sweat. Not a sight that would normally make her heart beat faster.

'Sorry. I remember my grandmother telling me you never call a gentleman by his first name until you've been properly introduced.'

'We had tea together last night, so I think we've been properly introduced. How long are you staying here?'

The question took her by surprise, but the stop at the lake had been unplanned. 'I'm not sure. I'm on my way to stay with my aunt but I can't seem to contact her. She's quite an active person, so she's out a lot. I want to make sure she's expecting us. Her memory isn't as good as it used to be.' Most of that was the truth.

Theo stretched his arms above his head and Sara saw him wince. 'I'm here another week. I've been here nearly a month already. I'm supposed to be recuperating, but it can get somewhat boring. When my sister said this was the place for peace and quiet, she wasn't joking. There's an old couple in the first cabin, but all he talks about is fishing, a subject I know absolutely nothing about, and his wife doesn't say much at all. At the other end we have a couple of enthusiastic hikers. They left at the crack of dawn this morning. The cabin next to yours on the other side is empty at the moment, but probably not for long. I was told the cabins are usually fully booked.'

'So I was lucky to get one. Jake will love it here. I'll probably have to drag him away when we leave.' She looked at her son and laughed. He was running up and down the path being chased by a very happy little dog. 'I think he's fallen in love with Rosie.'

'Jake doesn't have a dog?'

She shook her head. 'No. I work, and he's in preschool, so it's not practical. Maybe one day.' She knew she sounded wistful and that wouldn't do. She had to stay cheerful for Jake's sake. 'I have no idea how much the cabin costs to rent. That might make a difference to how long we stay.'

'Not too bad this early in the year. The rent is by the week, so you might as well get your money's worth.'

He sounded as if he was encouraging her to stay, probably because he wanted someone to talk to. She didn't intend doing much talking, she just needed to keep her head down until she could get in touch with her aunt.

'Jake needs his breakfast,' she said. 'I'd better get him back inside before he wears himself out.' She called out to Jake, who reluctantly gave the dog one last pat and started back towards his mother.

'I've got a ball somewhere inside,' Theo Winter said. 'I'll see if I can find it. Next time you play with Rosie, Jake, you can throw the ball for her.'

Jake ran up the steps. 'Can I, Mummy? Please.'

Sara felt she was being manoeuvred, but there wasn't much she could do except nod. As long as Jake didn't leave her sight, there shouldn't be a problem.

'I don't know how long we'll be staying here, Jake.'

'But we'll be here a little bit, won't we? We don't have to go soon.'

Sara gave up. 'No, we don't have to go soon,' she told him. 'Not right away. And you can play with Rosie again if Mr Winter . . . Theo . . . says so.'

She took Jake's hand but he dug his heels in, refusing to move. 'And will you take me on the boat? I've never been on a boat.'

Theo laughed. 'I'll find out if the boat's safe and then we'll see.' He looked at Sara. 'The boat's tied to a post with a pretty hefty-looking rope, so I'm sure it's safe, but I'll check it out. Let me know when you decide how long you'll be staying.'

She promised she would, and dragged her reluctant son back inside, making sure she locked the door onto the deck.

She was rinsing the breakfast dishes in the sink when someone knocked on the front door. There would come a time, she told herself, when an unexpected knock on the door wouldn't send adrenaline pumping through her body so fast she felt lightheaded. But that time hadn't come yet. Jake was watching her, so she took a deep breath and smiled at him. It never worked, and he was still looking at her with big worried eyes, but it made her feel she was coping.

'I wonder who that is,' she said brightly. She wouldn't know until she opened the door, she knew that, but it was still hard to do. She opened the door, breathing a sigh of relief when she saw Gareth standing at the top of the steps.

'I brought you your welcome box. I'll put it on the kitchen counter, shall I?'

He was past her before she could stop him. He put the box on the worktop and turned to smile at her. He reminded her of a very young Hugh Grant, and she imagined he had plenty of girlfriends already.

'Thank you. I only intend staying a day or two, but I need to know your mother's rates for the cabin.'

'The rent is £50 a day at this time of the year. There's no really big fish in the lake, only small stuff, so we're not fully booked yet. Mum says you can pay as you go along, if you like, or pay £300 for the week. That way you get a free day.' He took a sheet of paper from the top of the box. 'If you want to pay by card, you'll have to come up to the house.'

'No.' She knew she had answered a little too quickly, but her card was only for emergencies. 'No, thank you. I'll give you a couple of days' rent now. I have to get in touch with a relative, and then I'll know how long I'll be staying.' She took her son's hand. 'Jake, this is Gareth. He's brought us a box of groceries. You can help me put them away in a minute.' She turned back to Gareth. 'Let me pay you for three days to be going on with. By then I should be able to tell you exactly how long we'd like to stay.' She took her purse from her bag and counted out £150 in notes. 'That saves messing about with credit cards.'

He took the money, rolled it up and stuffed it in a pocket of his jeans. 'You can phone Mum if you need anything. The phone number is on the receipt.'

He wrote the amount on the sheet of paper and handed it back to her.

'That's fine. I have a mobile phone with me. Thanks again, Gareth.'

There were always so many questions, she thought as she closed the door after him. They probably shouldn't have stopped anywhere, but the storm had been really bad and she didn't want to descend on her aunt without warning. The last time she had seen Aunt Marjory had been at her parents' funeral, and she hadn't been pregnant then. Turning up out of the blue with a child in tow might seem a trifle presumptuous. Her aunt had kept in touch by email, and Sara always replied, but she had never mentioned Jake. She wasn't sure why. Perhaps because she wanted her aunt to think she was still the ambitious career girl she used to be. She wasn't ashamed of being a single parent, quite the contrary, but she couldn't face pity in any of its forms.

She took out her mobile phone and

dialled her aunt again, wondering if she had the right number. She might have to risk emailing. Perhaps she was being paranoid, but she thought people might be able to track her via her emails. The mobile phone seemed safer. There was still no reply, and she left yet another message asking her aunt to phone her back.

Jake was sitting on the sofa, not exactly sulking but not happy with her either. He'd wanted to stay and play with the dog, and even his favourite breakfast cereal hadn't made up for her dragging him back inside.

'Mid-morning snack?' she suggested cheerfully. Ignoring Jake's sulks usually worked. He didn't have a lot of stamina when it came to sulking. When she was a child, she'd managed to keep a sulk up for hours.

He looked up at her cautiously. 'What kind of snack?'

'I can give you a banana, or . . . how about a cupcake?'

'With frosting on top?'

'With frosting on top.' She had found the cupcakes in the box Gareth had left on the counter. They looked home-made, probably by his mother, unless Gareth was more talented than she had imagined. She hadn't seen any sign of a Mr Cartwright and wondered if there was one. Apart from the cupcakes and a pack of digestive biscuits, there was a bottle of washing-up liquid, a scouring pad, milk, teabags and a small loaf of fresh bread. If they were going to survive for three days, she was going to have to find a supermarket, which would probably mean driving to a nearby village. She wished Felicity Cartwright had included a bottle of wine in the box.

This time, when the doorbell sounded, she didn't jump quite as much.

3

'I came bearing gifts,' Theo said. 'Well, at least one gift.' He handed her a bottle of Sancerre, which made her laugh.

'Funnily enough, I was thinking how nice a glass of wine would taste, but it's a little early in the day.'

'Not when you're on holiday, and not if you dilute the wine with ice cubes.' He was already unscrewing the bottle top. 'I think it's warm enough to sit out on your deck. Jake can play with Rosie. She brought her ball with her this time.'

It might be sunny, but it was still quite early in the year. Sara made sure Jake was zipped up in his jacket before she realised what she was doing. The man had a very persuasive way about him, and that could be dangerous.

He banged the ice cube tray on the counter top and scooped the cubes into glasses he'd already half-filled with wine, and before she knew what had happened she was sitting beside him on the sunny deck while Jake threw a yellow tennis ball for Rosie. Theo stretched his long legs out in front of him, took a sip of his wine, and sighed with satisfaction. 'Some people would say it's criminal to dilute this wine, but I'm not one of those people.' He looked at her over the top of his glass. 'So, how's it going?'

'Fine.' Sara felt her stomach clench, sure he was going to ask her questions she didn't want to answer. 'But if we're going to stay a couple more days, I need to get some food. Is there a shop near here?'

'In the village. It's walking distance for grownups but probably not for Jake. Do you have a buggy with you?'

She laughed. 'You are joking, I hope. Try asking Jake how he feels about sitting in a buggy. That's if you dare.'

'What was I thinking? The boy is four years old, nearly five. I should know better.' Theo turned to watch Jake field the ball with one foot before it reached the water. 'And a budding footballer with that much talent should never be made to ride in a baby-buggy.'

'No problem. I'll take the car if you point me in the right direction.' She hesitated, wondering if she was being foolish, but then thought to hell with it. 'If I keep the rest of the wine for later, may I cook dinner for you tonight? Nothing fancy, just to say thank you for being so helpful — and for the wine, of course.'

He smiled at her as he got to his feet. 'That would be nice. I have some work to do, but Jake can borrow Rosie for a bit. It seems a shame to spoil their fun. Tell him to knock on my door when he's had enough and I'll let her back in.'

She told Jake he had ten more minutes, which seemed to be the only amount of time he understood, and watched Theo walk back to his cabin. Why on earth had she done something so daft?

All she had to do was maintain a low profile for a couple of days. Inviting a strange man to dinner wasn't exactly keeping a low profile. Give Theo time and he would want to know all about her, a subject that would fill a good-sized book. She took her eyes off Jake for a moment to put the wine in the refrigerator and top her glass up with some of Jake's orange juice, and then went back outside to sit in the sunshine and watch her son enjoying himself.

It wasn't until that moment she realised Theo had volunteered absolutely nothing about himself. She had found in the past that men usually wanted to talk about themselves. What they did for a living, what their hobbies were, what music they listened to and what they liked to eat. Theo had told her he was recuperating from an accident, but that was all. She knew as little about him as he did about her. Less, in fact.

She called to Jake as he headed towards the water after the ball. It looked shallow enough, but even though he couldn't swim yet he wasn't afraid of the water. She didn't want to have to go in after him. She wondered if the little path she could see went all the way round the lake. That would be a lovely walk, one that Jake would be able to manage. She could always give him a piggyback if he got tired. She had done that many times. It was one of the joys of single parenthood. He was too heavy now to perch on her hip like he used to, so she had to improvise.

Twenty minutes later, the dog had collapsed in the shade and Jake was splashing in the shallows, his shorts already soaked. There was always the chance of a sudden drop off beneath the waterline, and she feared he might disappear from sight before she could get to him. She called to him, annoyed with herself for daydreaming. At least he'd had the sense to take his shoes off.

'Go and knock on Mr Winter's door so he can call Rosie. I'll watch you from here.'

Jake pulled at the legs of his shorts. 'I'm all wet.'

'That's your fault for not doing what you were told. Don't go near the water again without asking. Understand? And put your shoes back on.'

She watched him struggle to do so on wet feet. Dying to help him, she took a deep breath. His fault, she told herself, so he had to suffer a little. Maybe he wouldn't do it again. *Fat chance*, she thought with a smile as he called Rosie and plodded up the steps to Theo's front door.

She heard someone call out behind her and turned to see a small white-haired lady waving a tentative hand. 'I only wanted to say hello. I'm June. June Nightingale. We're staying in the first cabin. It's lovely here, isn't it? We come every year to get away from the noise of the town for a while, and so Harry can do some fishing. He's not very good, so he never catches anything, but it's fun to watch him try.' The woman turned to look at Jake as he knocked on Theo's door. 'Your little boy is gorgeous; he's about the same age as our grandson.'

Theo opened his door and shooed Rosie inside. 'Hi, June,' he called. 'How's Harry?'

'Still feeling sorry for himself,' the woman called back. 'I drove him all the way to casualty and nothing's broken. Silly man should look where he's going.' She turned to Sara. 'My foolish husband turned round to talk to me and fell off the deck. I told him it serves him right for always wanting the last word.' She frowned. 'I came over to tell you something, but I've forgotten what it was. Oh, I know. I saw your little boy paddling in the lake and I thought I'd let you know the lake is quite shallow by the cabins. It's shingle on the bottom and only about a foot deep. It might hurt his feet but he won't suddenly disappear from sight. Our two grandchildren join us here sometimes, so I know how worrying children and water can be.'

Only another mother would under-stand the constant worry of being responsible for a child. Particularly a four-year-old boy. Sara thought grand-parenting probably had its ups and downs. A big responsibility when you were in charge of a small child, but great fun. Particularly when you could hand him back at the end of a tiring day. Something her own parents would never have to worry about. Sara wished her mother had lived long enough to know what it was like to be a grandmother. She would have been great at it.

'I'll see you later,' Theo called to her before he shut the door, and Sara flushed as June gave her a knowing smile.

'He's nice, isn't he?' the woman said. 'He's got some sort of injury. Have you noticed the way he limps? He says he's come here to recuperate, but he spends a lot of his time outside walking his dog. He told me he's writing a book about his experiences.'

'Is he?' Sara was intrigued. 'What sort of experiences?'

'I don't know, dear. He didn't tell me, but I'm sure it's something exciting.'

Like six months in a high-security prison, Sara thought. *Or how he overcame alcoholism.* There were a lot of possibilities. He didn't look the sort to collect stamps or keep a butterfly collection. But having enough experiences to fill a book — that was interesting. Maybe she could ask him later.

Jake was back. He stood at the bottom of the steps looking at June Nightingale curiously. 'Do you live here?'

'Yes, dear. We live in the end cabin. Next door but one to you and your mummy.'

'Near the boat?'

'Jake, stop asking questions.' Sara took his hand and led him up the steps. 'Don't go near that boat without permission. OK?'

'We were told it's for the use of the residents,' June said. 'But Harry can't even manage the steps without falling over, so I can't imagine what he would be like in a boat. It would be a disaster.' She gave Sara a sly smile. 'Theo might take you out for a row if you ask him nicely. There's nothing wrong with his arms.'

She trotted off back to her cabin before Sara could think of a retort.

*　*　*

Sara found the village without any trouble. It was only ten minutes away by car in spite of the state of the road, but by the time she had parked, Jake was nodding off in his car seat. She turned the radio on to wake him up and then sat in the car looking around to get her bearings. She didn't intend staying in the village longer than absolutely necessary.

She could see the supermarket across the road, a small Tesco Express, and a bank on the corner. She needed money but she couldn't decide where to get it. She could use her card to ask for cash back, or she could go to the bank. If she chose the bank, she wouldn't have to put her card in a machine, she could hand it over the counter and ask for money. That way, no one would see it except the counter clerk. She'd been caught once before using an ATM, so she didn't do that anymore. An ATM often had a security camera watching it.

Having decided on the bank, she helped a still-sleepy Jake out of the car and walked across the road. She withdrew £200 and headed for the supermarket. Her bank account was still fairly healthy, but now the money from her job had stopped coming in she would eventually run out of funds. Not something she was going to worry about yet, though.

The thought of shopping for food was quite exciting, particularly when you had an attractive man to feed; and Theo was attractive, there was no denying that. What did he do that was interesting enough to write about? she wondered. And was his injury related to his job? He didn't look like an intrepid explorer, someone who had been attacked by a lion. He didn't look much like a member of the SAS, either, but that was a distinct possibility because she had no idea what a member of the SAS would look like. The ones she had seen had been wearing balaclavas.

Amused by her flight of fancy, she was almost back to her car with her shopping before she noticed the man standing outside the bank. He attracted her attention because he looked as if he was going hiking. He had on thick boots and a rucksack on his back, a peaked cap was pulled down over his face, and he was wearing an anorak, which looked a little incongruous on a warm spring day. She strapped Jake into his seat and got in herself, but she didn't immediately start the engine. The man probably had an appointment with the bank manager. But if so, why was he hanging around outside? Looking for somebody, maybe? She shook her head and turned the key in the ignition. Now she really was getting paranoid.

'Don't go to sleep in the car again,' she told Jake. 'I want you to sleep in your bed tonight.'

As she turned the car around she saw the man walk into the bank, and she relaxed enough to start thinking about her dinner menu. Spaghetti Bolognaise had been her first choice, but that was so predictable she dismissed it straight away. She wanted to make something interesting that wouldn't look as if she was trying too hard to impress, and she was finding that difficult because the cooking facilities in the cabin were restricted. The oven looked OK, and there were two electric hotplates, but she didn't intend faffing about making pastry; the frozen stuff would have to do. Her menu now consisted of salmon quiche made with ready-cooked salmon and a pack of fresh farm eggs, rocket for a side salad, and baked apple with double cream for dessert. Simple but effective, she hoped. The remainder of the Sancerre, nicely chilled but without the ice, should suit her menu perfectly.

She managed to keep Jake awake long enough to feed him, and then popped him into bed. She had a feeling he was asleep before she closed the door. This had been his most active day since she took him out of school. Only preschool, admittedly, but quite important when big school loomed in a little over four months' time. Somehow she had to get her life sorted before then and register Jake for a local school. She also needed to find another job, and that wasn't going to be easy without a reference. If she still couldn't contact her aunt in a couple of days' time, she would have to continue her journey to Norfolk and hope for the best. She knew Aunt Marjory was expecting her, but she hadn't been able to give a definite date.

She wanted to change before Theo arrived, but she didn't have much choice where clothes were concerned. She had vacuum-packed most of her clothes and left them in her friend's loft in London, and all she had with her were decidedly crumpled. She found an iron in one of the kitchen cupboards and smoothed the creases in a silk blouse. The pale blue silk looked pretty good over her dark jeans, and once she had added lipstick and mascara she felt in much better shape to face The Ice Man.

He was bang on time. Sara opened the door knowing she was making a big mistake, but she had eaten alone so often recently that the thought of company, any company, had been too tempting. She had lived by herself for five years, and in that time she had made a lot of friends. Her life had been pretty good. But that life had suddenly disappeared and she had done the only thing possible at the time. She had packed their bags and taken off into the unknown.

Theo handed her another bottle of Sancerre. 'I thought we might run out.'

Was he hoping to get her drunk? 'This is a meal to say thank you, Theo,' she told him. 'Nothing more.'

He looked puzzled for a minute, and then he grinned. 'Shucks, that's completely spoiled my evening. I might as well turn around and go home.'

Sara felt her face go hot with embarrassment. 'Sorry.' She took the bottle and stood back from the door. 'Please come in. I was beginning to think it was a bit forward of me to invite you to dinner when I hardly know you, and I didn't want you to get any ideas, but that was rude of me.'

'No problem. I wouldn't be a red-blooded male if I didn't get ideas, but I have no intention of following up on any of them. Not tonight, anyway.' He gave her another grin. 'Having got that out of the way, may I pour you a glass of wine?'

Not the best way to start the evening, she thought. Now there was a rather large elephant in the room, and that was all her fault. 'Yes, please,' she said meekly. 'I'll go and check on the food.'

She liked watching him eat. It was a long time since she'd watched a man eat at her table, and she found she was enjoying it. He finished up the quiche and devoured his apple with obvious relish.

'I've never had an apple done like this before. It's unbelievably good.'

She smiled with pleasure. 'Sometimes the simple things are the best. A Bramley apple stuffed with raisins, drizzled with honey, and then baked in the oven.'

She'd only got instant coffee, but topped up with the remains of the cream it wasn't too bad. Theo helped her clear the table, but she waved away his offer of help with the washing up. 'I'll cover everything with water and do it in the morning. No rush. Sit down and enjoy your coffee. Mrs Nightingale said you're writing a book, and I wondered what it was about.' She tried to make it sound casual, but it came out like the start of the Spanish Inquisition. 'Sorry. None of my business if you don't want to talk about it.'

He was silent for a moment, just looking at her. 'Why do you keep apologising? If you want to know something, there's never any harm in asking, but it goes both ways. If I tell you what my book is about, will you tell me what you're running away from?'

If it was that obvious, she didn't stand much chance. She tried a casual smile. 'You are assuming, Mr Winter, and it never pays to assume. Besides, I don't want to spoil your evening with the story of my life. It's my fault for poking my nose in where it's not wanted, and I should know better. But you are a clever man. You backed me into a corner.'

'My job,' he said. 'I'm a lawyer.'

Suddenly the name clicked into place. 'Of course! Theodore Winter. The

Ice Man. You were in the news a little while ago, weren't you? You got shot on the steps of the courthouse.' That explained the limp.

'I got shot for poking my nose in where it's not wanted. Sometimes it pays to myob.'

'Myob?'

'Mind your own business,' he said with a smile. 'But unfortunately it's my job to ask questions, and I'm naturally curious by nature.'

She closed her eyes, thinking back, and then opened them wide. 'Now I remember. It was on the television news. They were filming you coming out of the courthouse after some important case. I was only half watching but the noise of the gunshot was so unexpected it made me jump. I thought you were dead. You went down like — '

'A lawyer who had just managed to get a guilty verdict reversed. Perks of the job.'

'I don't think many lawyers get shot.

It was the father of a girl who'd been killed by a hit-and-run driver who shot you, wasn't it? I can't really say I blame him. You stopped her killer going to prison.'

'Her killer was a fourteen-year-old kid who'd taken his father's car for a joy ride and then got chased by the police. He was scared witless. That doesn't excuse him, but it doesn't warrant ten years in a juvenile detention centre. The judge was making him an example, 'To stop the same thing happening again' he said.'

Sara thought of Jake and his lack of road sense. 'But I can imagine how the father must have felt. He lost his daughter.'

'And the parents of the boy would have lost a son. He would have been twenty-four by the time he got out. Two wrongs don't always make a right.'

She smiled. 'I'm not going to agree with what you did, but you got punished for your sins so I'm inclined to let you off. How bad is your leg?'

'From your point of view, about right I should think. It took the surgeon a bit of hunting around to find the bullet, so there's quite a lot of muscle damage. It hurts like hell most of the time, but the leg's getting better. I went home after my stay in hospital and had the whole family fussing around, trying to keep me off my feet, so I came out here to write. A publisher had already commissioned a book. It's fiction, by the way, not my life story.'

'Like John Grisham. You must have lots of stories to tell.'

'I do. That's why it's fiction. I don't want to get sued.'

'That would be fun, wouldn't it? A battle of the lawyers. Fantastic publicity.'

'If you like publicity, which I don't. I imagine you don't, either.'

Sara desperately tried to think of a way to change the subject. She'd known this was going to happen. There were always questions. She should have learnt her lesson by now. She was saved from having to answer when a car door slammed right outside. The knock on the door that followed sent a shot of adrenalin through her veins, and she felt the familiar sickness in the pit of her stomach.

Theo must have seen the fear on her face, even though she did her best to hide it. He got to his feet. 'Stay where you are,' he said quietly. 'I'll get the door.'

She wanted to run and hide in the bedroom with Jake, but she leant back on the sofa and tried to look like a girl who was having a fun evening with a dishy man. He couldn't have found her already. She had been too careful. Probably Mrs Nightingale wanting to borrow a cup of sugar.

But when Theo opened the door, the figure on the step definitely wasn't Mrs Nightingale. She watched the man's eyes flick disinterestedly past her and scan the rest of the room. She hoped it was only curiosity. There was nowhere to hide, so she got to her feet and moved slowly across the floor to join

Theo. The man was dressed in a leather jacket and jeans with what looked like new boots on his feet. He was around his mid-forties, she guessed, with dark hair and a round face. A baseball cap sat on his head facing backwards. There was nothing particularly memorable about him, but she had a curious feeling she had seen him before.

'Sorry to bother you at this hour,' the man said. 'I'm looking for cabin number two. It's bloody dark out here.'

'It's next to this one.' Theo glanced over the man's shoulder at his car, a scruffy-looking silver Vauxhall. 'There's parking beside the cabin.'

'Thanks. Name's Kevin. Kevin Spender. Here for the fishing.' He lifted a hand to Sara and trotted back down the steps.

Theo shut the door and turned to look at her. 'He's gone. A fisherman come for a bit of sport, nothing more. Do you want to tell me what's going on?'

She shook her head. She felt incredibly tired. 'Not right now, but thank you for coming round. It's been a really nice evening.'

He stood for a moment, looking at her. 'I'll put on my lawyer's voice and say it sometimes helps to talk to someone. If there's money involved, or any other kind of legalities, I might be able to help. I need to keep my hand in, so I'm more than happy to take your case pro bono. That's if you have a case, of course. As I told you before, I'm bored out of my mind doing nothing. I need a bit of excitement.'

'Like getting shot at?'

He stood quite still in the centre of the room, as if considering. 'Is that likely to happen?' When she didn't answer, he smiled. 'Even if it is, the offer still stands.' He walked towards the door. 'Fate moves in mysterious ways, Sara; and if a lawyer might be able to help you, you've landed in exactly the right place at exactly the right time. At this particular moment you're living next door to The Ice Man.'

4

Before Theo went back to his cabin, he checked on number two. The silver car was parked on the hard standing, and a light was on behind the curtained window. He stood looking at the cabin for a moment. Something about Kevin Spender didn't quite ring true, and Theo was used to making a quick judgement of character. A definite necessity on a courtroom floor.

He walked slowly back the way he had come and let himself in, bending down to stroke Rosie as she pranced at his feet, delighted with his return. He turned on the lights and looked round the room. His cabin was furnished with the same furniture and fittings as Sara's, even down to the kitchen equipment and cushions on the sofa, so why did it look so different? It could be the candles she'd put on the dinner table, or maybe the toys he'd noticed piled in a corner, but her room had a warmth to it that his didn't. And she'd managed to add that warmth in just one day.

Shrugging, he went into his bedroom, unbuckled the leather belt holding up his jeans, slid them down over his hips and stepped out of them. With slippers on his feet instead of trainers, he went back into the living room and picked up his laptop. Settling himself on the sofa clad in boxer shorts and vest, he turned on the computer and Googled Kevin Spender.

A few seconds later he had several hits. So the man did actually exist; that was something. Theo wouldn't have been surprised if his Google search had come up empty. Kevin Spender was CEO for Spender Investigations, Ltd, a company based in Leeds. But when Theo tried to find out what sort of investigations the company carried out, everything became a bit vague. There was, however, a Leeds telephone number. Too late tonight, but something he could chase up tomorrow. Investigations sounded suspiciously like a posh label for a sleazy detective agency. Sara was worried about something, and if she was being followed it would be a bit of a coincidence for a private investigator to accidentally rent a cabin next door to her.

He got up from his chair and found the bottle of brandy he'd bought in the village a couple of days ago. Unscrewing the cap, he poured a shot into one of the wine glasses that came with the cabin. The next best thing to a brandy snifter, he supposed, although in his opinion a good brandy tasted exactly the same from of a plastic cup. Sitting back down on the sofa, he stretched his long legs out in front of him and thought about little miss Sara Finch. She was running from something, or someone; and if he'd been in a courtroom he could have extracted the information from her in a couple of minutes. But he wasn't in a courtroom. He took a sip of his brandy.

Kevin Spender probably had nothing whatsoever to do with Sara Finch's problem. Perhaps he really was on an innocent fishing trip. But there was still something about the man that rang alarm bells. Theo tried to work out what had started those bells ringing. Nothing specific, just a lot of little things. The hiking boots were new. OK if you were going hiking, but not really necessary or suitable for a fishing trip. The jacket looked like leather, but it was decidedly shabby. So was the car; and Spender didn't look the sort of man to come on a fishing trip on his own. If he was a serious fisherman, or even a beginner wanting to learn about the sport, why come on his own and out of season? Theo made a mental note to check the registration number of the car in daylight. It looked like a Vauxhall, but it was difficult to tell in the dark.

He slept better than he had for a long time. Probably because he was using his brain again. Boredom always kept him awake at night. He hadn't remembered to take any medication for his leg, and he had only woken up once. On his way back from the bathroom he had quickly checked to make sure Sara's cabin was dark and quiet, but once he was satisfied she was in no danger, he had gone straight back to sleep again. Usually, if he got up in the night, his leg kept him awake until he swallowed another painkiller.

He awoke at six-thirty feeling rested and more like his old self. After a quick breakfast of toast and coffee, he was out walking Rosie by seven. The usual mist hung over the lake, the water black and still. They had only gone a little way down the path when Rosie disturbed a water vole. Often called a water rat, the vole was a lot prettier than a rat. This little fellow had chubby cheeks, neat little ears, and a hairy tail. The vole scuttled quickly away, disappearing into an almost invisible hole in the bank, a hole too small for Rosie to get her nose inside even though she tried. She ran back to Theo, shaking her head and snorting.

'Serves you right if you sniffed up a load of soil,' he told her. 'You could have had your nose bitten off.'

He usually took the left-hand path, which veered off into a small copse of assorted trees and bushes, because Rosie loved rooting amongst the trees. But today he went to the right, past Sara's cabin and on to the one Spender now occupied. The curtains were still drawn across the windows, but at least Theo could get a good look at the car. He had been right about the make: the car was a nondescript silver Vauxhall. About six years old, judging by the number plate. As he wandered nonchalantly past cabin number two, he made a mental note of the car's registration so he could check it later. He didn't need to write it down. He had a particularly good memory.

He called to Rosie, who was exploring the river bank, and walked on down the path towards the boat sitting on the shingle. He quite fancied taking Jake out for a row across the lake, but Sara seemed a little overprotective, and he wasn't sure what she would think of his plan. On closer inspection, the boat looked watertight, apart from a puddle in the bottom left from the storm, and in good condition. A couple of oars rested in the rowlocks. He decided he might take the boat out anyway. Rosie had never been in a boat and he was sure she'd love it.

Someone had cleared the lane the day after the storm, and most of the path was free of debris, but Theo found he still had to watch where he put his feet. He glanced at his watch, wondering if Gareth or his mother would be up and about this early in the morning. As he approached the house, a face peered out of one of the downstairs windows, and he waved a hand in greeting.

Felicity Cartwright met him at the front door. She was a slim woman, most probably in her mid-forties, wearing jeans and a pale pink sweater, her hair a wild mess of unruly curls. 'Hello, Theo. What can I do for you?' She bent down to pet Rosie, who wriggled with delight. 'Nothing wrong, I hope.'

Theo smiled at her. 'What could be wrong on a lovely morning like this? I wanted to ask about the boat. I was thinking about taking Sara Finch's little boy for a row across the lake, if his mother agrees.'

'You can use the outboard if you want, it's quite easy to fit, but rowing is more fun. The outboard scares the wildlife. There are a lot of fish in the lake, and there are also otters and some quite rare water birds.'

'And voles. Rosie tried to catch one this morning, but it was too quick for her. She stuck her head in its nest and got mud up her nose.'

Felicity tutted. 'Poor baby. Dogs hate to be humiliated. Yes, of course you can take the boat. Any time you want. Just pull it up out of the water when you get back and tie it up again. Miss Finch seems a nice young lady, but the storm was in full force when she arrived and she didn't have time to chat. She was wet through and she wanted to get to her cabin and put her little boy to bed.'

She wasn't the only one who had finished up wet through, Theo thought. 'You have a new guest, apart from Sara Finch,' he said casually. 'A fisherman, I believe. He apparently had trouble finding his cabin.'

'That's strange. I gave him good directions and told him it was the second cabin along.' Felicity shrugged. 'Oh, well, he obviously found it in the end. He said he might have a friend arriving, another fisherman, but no one has arrived so far. He wanted to know if there would be room for his friend to have his own cabin.'

Theo took a minute to think about that. It was a good way to find out how many cabins were actually occupied. If Spender was looking for Sara, he hadn't seemed particularly interested in her, but that in itself was odd. She had dressed up for their meal and looked stunning.

Feigning disinterest, he said, 'He probably won't stay if his friend doesn't turn up. Not much fun fishing on your own, I wouldn't think.'

She smiled. 'I have more non-fishermen than fishermen here at the moment, what with you and Sara Finch. How's your leg? Better, I hope.'

'Much better, thank you. I'll have to think about going home soon. Maybe in another few days. I've been idle long enough.'

'We'll miss you, Theo. Have fun with the boat.'

Sara was standing on her deck trying to get a signal on her phone when Theo came back along the path with Rosie. The dog galloped over to push her nose through the bars of the rail, and Sara bent to scratch her head.

'Problem?' Theo asked.

She held up her phone. 'Any idea how I can get a decent signal? I'm still trying to contact my aunt.'

'It all depends on your service provider. You could ask to use the phone in the house. I'm sure they won't mind.'

'Which is the easiest to trace? A landline or a mobile?'

'Probably the landline, because there's something called a reverse directory. Apart from that, the police can trace a call on any landline where the number is registered, like here. But your mobile phone can be traced as well if someone has the technology.' He looked down at Rosie. 'Give me ten minutes to feed the dog and then come over. Jake can play with her and you can use my phone. I seem to have a pretty good signal.'

'Want to go and play with Rosie?' Sara asked Jake, smiling at his enthusiastic response.

'Yay! Can I throw the ball? Can I take her for a walk?'

'No going for walks. You'll stay right outside the cabin or no more games with the dog. Understood? Thank you, Theo. We'll be over in a little while.'

Theo wondered why she kept Jake on such a tight leash; she seemed scared to let him out of her sight. It would be good if the boy was allowed to explore, he couldn't come to much harm out here. Theo remembered playing in the woods with his older brother when he was about six years old and not getting back until dark. It was different, he supposed, when you were an only child, and Jake wasn't quite five years old yet.

Sara turned up with biscuits and a covered mug of juice for Jake. She thanked Theo again and took his phone out on to the veranda. He saw her pacing, looking anxiously at the dial, obviously not getting an answer.

'No reply?'

'No, and I'm getting a bit worried now. I let the phone ring until the automatic answer service picked up and left a message. I was trying not to sound desperate because I didn't want to worry my aunt unduly, but I really need her to answer. She knows we're coming, but not exactly when.' She handed Theo back his phone. 'Thanks again. I don't know what to do now. I think I'll have to drive to the village in Norfolk and try and find my aunt's house.'

'You don't know her address?' It seemed strange Sara didn't know where her aunt lived.

'She's my aunty,' Sara said defensively. 'My mother's older sister. The only relative I have left. The only blood relative, anyway. I know the name of the village but not the exact house. I expect everyone knows everyone in a small village so someone will be able to tell me.' She took a sip of the tea she had made for both of them and watched Jake throw the ball for Rosie. 'He's so happy here, it would be nice to stay for longer. Like a proper holiday.'

She hadn't answered his question, but he let it go for now. 'Why are you so desperate to visit your aunt? You must have a home somewhere.'

She shook her head. 'No, we don't. At the moment we have nowhere to live. I was looking for another flat because our landlord kept raising the rent, then I lost my job. There was no way I could afford any sort of rent without a job. My landlord wouldn't refund my deposit, and he refused to give me a reference so I could rent somewhere else. Then I got a visit from a charity that helps homeless families. She said they had been informed I was about to lose my flat, and if I had nowhere to go the charity would find me a room in a shelter where I could take proper care of my child. I told her I had family who would help me, but she didn't believe me. I have a pretty good idea who informed them I was going to become homeless.'

'You should have gone to social services and explained. They would have helped you find a job and a place to live.' He took a bottle of brandy out of a cupboard. 'You need a shot of something in that tea.'

He hadn't realised how near she was to tears, but now her eyes filled and she brushed a hand across her face. 'I don't do this normally. I don't cry. I can't, not in front of Jake. He thinks this is all a big adventure, but I have to get him booked into a school somewhere. He's supposed to start in September.' She took a big gulp of her tea and nearly choked. 'I thought you said a drop of brandy, not half a cup.' She stood up to get her breath back, laughing and crying at the same time, and without thinking he put his arms round her. She rested her head on his shoulder for a moment and he could smell her shampoo, something flowery and spicy at the same time, and then she disentangled herself and moved away from him. 'Now I feel really ridiculous.'

The feel of her in his arms had been nice. 'I have a sister,' he said. 'She's a girl, so she cries a lot.'

'I don't.'

'Then make the most of it. A good cry sometimes helps. No sense in bottling it all up.'

She sat down on the sofa and picked up her cup. She took a small sip this time. 'If I'm going to cry all over your shirt, I probably owe you an explanation.'

'You don't owe me anything. But if you want to talk, I'm available.' He glanced out of the window. 'And Jake is happy playing with Rosie.' He watched her take a breath, either to marshal her thoughts or settle her nerves. Whatever she was going to tell him was proving harder than she had expected.

'I don't know where to start.'

'The beginning is probably as good a place as any.'

She looked at Jake, who was now running round in circles waving a stick while Rosie chased him enthusiastically. 'My parents died five years ago. They died together in a car accident. I was twenty-three and about to graduate from university, but I didn't know how to manage without them.' Another breath. 'The funeral was a nightmare. Nobody knew what to say to me. The only person who talked to me was my mother's sister — my aunt Marjory. She said my parents had spoken to her often on the phone, and they were very proud of me. She told me if I ever needed help, to go to her. She's in her sixties, but she's still up to date with all the new technology. She has a computer and she gave me her email address.'

'So you kept in touch?'

Sara kept her head down, looking at the floor. 'Sort of. When I met her at the funeral, I had a job offer lined up, a nice flat, and I was dating a rich boy I met at university. She told me she was proud of me. Then I got pregnant and stopped emailing her.'

She glanced up, but he didn't say anything so she carried on.

'After I had Jake, I didn't want to go straight back to work full-time. I wanted to be with my baby. Besides, I couldn't afford the day care. My flat was big enough for both of us, and I had a degree in business management. I managed to get a job with a local insurance company, mostly working from home. They paid me well, and up until recently we were doing fine.'

Theo filled up her cup with hot tea and added a drop more brandy. 'What about Jake's father?'

She tried a smile, but it didn't really work. He was pretty sure she was about to answer, but a sudden movement down by the lake caught his eye. Then Rosie started barking at something in the bushes. The dog was making little rushes at something in the thick foliage at the edge of the water, barking furiously. Jake had stopped running; he was still holding tight to his stick but now he was looking a little scared. The bushes began to shake in earnest, and Theo wondered what sort of animal would make that much of a disturbance. Whatever it was, it was something pretty big.

He got to his feet. 'Rosie! Come here!'

Sara called to Jake to come back to the cabin. 'What is it?' she asked nervously.

The dog took no notice of Theo, and he hurried down the steps towards her. He had no idea what was hiding in the bushes, but there was no reason to frighten Sara or Jake until he found out. As he started down the bank he heard a muffled curse, then a splash, and Rosie's barking became almost frenzied. The little dog was standing with all four legs splayed, growling ominously. Theo had never seen her that freaked out before. Jake threw down his stick and ran back up the steps to stand beside his mother on the deck. She put her arm round him as a man emerged slowly from the foliage at the edge of the lake.

'Call the damned dog off. You should keep it locked up. It's dangerous.'

Theo caught up with Rosie and grabbed her by her collar. Kevin Spender emerged from the bushes covered in wet mud and various bits of greenery. He was holding a camera splashed with river water and looking distinctly annoyed. Theo hung on to

Rosie. She was pulling against her collar so fiercely her front feet were off the ground. She was making strangled noises at the back of her throat and baring her teeth at the fisherman.

'What the hell were you doing hiding in the bushes?'

Spender seemed to find Theo more menacing than the dog. He backed off a pace and nearly fell back into the lake. 'Trying to take some photos. No good now, though; you've probably ruined my camera.' He looked up at Theo, who was towering above him on the bank. 'Can you shut that dog up somewhere before it takes a piece out of me?'

'You'd better have a good explanation for skulking around or I might let her do just that. You frightened a little boy and nearly got yourself bitten by my dog. What were you trying to photograph that had you hiding in a bush?'

The man hesitated a beat too long. 'I was trying to get a shot of a bird. It's gone now, though.'

'I thought you were a fisherman, not a bird watcher.'

'A kingfisher. I was trying to photograph a kingfisher before it flew back up to its nest.' He picked a twig from his wet sweater and threw it on the ground. 'I always have a camera with me. If I catch a big fish in the lake tomorrow, I need a photo to prove it, don't I?' He eased his way past a still-grumbling Rosie and headed back towards his cabin. 'Look, I'm all wet. I need to go and change and see if my camera's still working. Sorry if I scared the kid.' Theo watched Spender walk back to his cabin and let himself in.

'What was that all about?' Sara asked.

'He said he was just taking a photo of a kingfisher as it flew back to its nest.'

'A kingfisher doesn't have a nest,' Jake said.

Sara looked down at her son in surprise while Theo hooted out a laugh. 'Brilliant, Jake! You're spot on.

Kingfishers don't make nests. Did you learn about that in school?'

'We had a book with pictures of birds. The kingfisher doesn't make a nest in a tree like other birds. It lives in a hole. Miss Robins said so.'

'And Miss Robins is exactly right.' Theo grinned at Jake. 'The kingfisher makes a nest on the bank of a lake or river, not in a tree. You knew something your mummy didn't know.'

'All the time,' Sara said with a laugh, but then her laugh died away. 'Do you think Mr Spender was lying? What else would he be doing hiding in a bush? He had a camera with him which is possibly ruined, thanks to Rosie.' She smiled a little shakily. 'Perhaps he'll sue your dog for malicious damage and you'll have to defend her in court. That would be fun, wouldn't it?' She took Jake's hand. 'Come on, young man, we must get back. It's nearly lunch time.'

Theo watched her until she was safely in her cabin, then he went inside with a still-excited Rosie.

'Calm down, girl. You did your bit. You scared Spender so much he fell in the water and ruined his photos.'

Theo was pretty sure the man hadn't been taking photos of birds, which left only one possibility: he had been taking photos of Sara Finch. There was, of course, a possibility that the man had Theo in his sights, but in that case he would more likely have been carrying a gun. Sara had been about to reveal her secret when the man had upset Rosie, and Theo knew it would be difficult to question her again. He was used to questioning people, but normally his interrogation took place in a cell or a courtroom.

Topping up his glass, he opened his laptop. The internet connection was surprisingly good away from the surrounding trees, but finding the right Sara Finch was slightly more difficult. She had no Facebook profile, and although there were a surprising number of women with the same name, none fitted Sara's age or occupation. He was guessing at her age, but it was possible to draw a timeline from what she had let slip accidentally and what she had told him. She had to be in her mid- to late twenties. Still a bit young for a cynical thirty-five-year-old, but that wasn't relevant at the moment.

5

While Sara busied herself preparing Jake's lunch, she tried to work out what she was going to do next. She felt emotionally drained. The fisherman had scared her. She couldn't imagine why he would lie, but she had seen the look on the man's face as he tried to think up a plausible excuse for hiding in the bushes. Theo obviously didn't believe the story either, and he was a lawyer. He must be used to distinguishing between a lie and the truth. As she put Jake's plate in front of him, he looked up at her worriedly.

'Why was that man hiding, Mummy? Is he a bad man?'

Sara shook her head, chiding herself for worrying her son. He had already been scared enough for one day. 'No, he's here for a holiday, like us. He dropped his camera when Rosie barked at him. That's why he was cross. I was thinking I'd seen him somewhere before.'

'I have,' Jake mumbled through a mouthful of cheese sandwich. Sara had been about to put the kettle on, but now she stopped and stared at her son.

'You've seen the fisherman before?'

Jake nodded. 'When I was in the car.' He took another bite of sandwich. 'I saw him out of the window.'

Sara closed her eyes. She knew she couldn't rush this. Jake's vocabulary was good for his age, but he didn't always make himself clear. 'While we've been here?' she said casually. 'While we've been at the cabin?'

'No. Like I said, when I was in the car. Can I have some juice, please?'

She poured juice into his special beaker and added a straw. 'Where, then?'

'I told you.' Jake gave her a look that said she was being particularly dense. 'When I was in the car. He was on the other side of the road.' Jake filled his mouth with juice and swallowed noisily. 'He went into the bank.'

Sara nodded. 'I remember now. He was wearing hiking boots.'

Jake rolled his eyes, a habit she must remember to speak to him about.

'And he had a bag, like a school bag.'

Sara nodded again. A backpack. Silently thanking her observant little son, she tried to stop the flutter of apprehension without much success. Had Spender followed them from London? No, he couldn't have. No one knew where they were going because she hadn't known herself. Pulling off the main road and renting a cabin had been a spur-of-the-moment thing, not something she had planned in advance. So no one knew where they were. It wasn't possible.

'I've eaten all my lunch. Can I go outside and play?'

'No,' she said sharply. She saw Jake's head come up.

'Why?'

She hadn't the heart to give him her

usual 'because I said so'. 'Give me ten minutes,' she told him. 'I need to check something on my laptop. Then we'll go for a walk and see if we can get all round the lake. Play with your Lego until I'm finished.'

She waited until Jake was settled and then turned on her computer. There was a chance that if the man wasn't who he said he was, he wouldn't show up when she Googled him. What had he said his first name was? A name she didn't particularly like. Brian? No, that wasn't it. Kevin, Kevin Spender. She typed in the name and looked at the list in front of her. One particular line jumped out at her. Spender Investigations. Feeling a little sick, she clicked on the name. Obligingly, there was a telephone number under the company name, together with a photograph of the CEO, but it wasn't the fisherman.

The man in the picture was white-haired and kindly-looking, unlike the bad-tempered Kevin, although their last names were the same. Either the fisherman had the same surname as the CEO of Spender Investigations purely by coincidence — which seemed rather unlikely — or the man in the picture was related to Kevin in some way, perhaps his father.

A private investigator turning up on her doorstep hadn't happened by chance. She wasn't naive enough to believe that. But if it wasn't a coincidence, what the hell was it?

Her immediate thought was to rush next door and tell Theo what she had found, but it occurred to her that she knew as little about Theo Winter as she did about Kevin Spender — maybe even less. No problem. A few more keystrokes gave her a page full of leads to Theodore Winter, Criminal Defence Lawyer, aka The Ice Man. She didn't want to read about his cases, some of them highly publicised. She wanted personal stuff. She smiled to herself as she clicked through the different options. Perhaps she should have clicked on a copy of Celebrity Gossip.

Theodore Winter wasn't married, and there was no mention of a current girlfriend. He had a mother, a father, and a sister who was married with a child and lived nearby. His parents had a house in Kent and ran the place as a smallholding, from what Sara could gather. Theo was 35 years old with a reputation as a coldly clinical defence lawyer who researched his cases meticulously and usually won. The police hated him because most of his work was helping the accused get off scot-free or receive a reduced sentence. A recent newspaper article suggested he should stop behaving like some sort of superhero and start upholding the law.

The photograph on her screen didn't look a bit like the man currently living next door. The Ice Man stood outside the Royal Courts of Justice in London looking straight into the camera. His eyes, which Sara would have described as silver, were a cold wintry grey, and the half-smile tipping the corner of his mouth was more cynical than amused. He was wearing a well-cut suit and had a leather document case under his arm. The epitome of a successful lawyer.

Sara sat back in her chair. Theodore Winter was an interesting man, but could she really trust him? She was beginning to wonder if she could trust anyone. If they stayed here much longer, they would be tracked down. It looked as if they probably had already. When money wasn't a problem, it was relatively easy to find someone, even if that someone didn't want to be found, and she didn't have anything like the resources the old man had. Which meant she might have to trust someone.

'Is that Theo?' Jake was standing behind her looking over her shoulder.

'Yes. He's a lawyer. He helps people stay out of prison.'

'Even if they've done something wrong?'

Sara wished she didn't have to answer that question. She liked to be truthful with her son. 'No, if they've done something really bad they still go to prison. The bad guys always get locked up.'

'I'm going to be a good guy when I grow up.'

She ruffled his hair. 'I'm glad to hear that. Now, do you still want to go for that walk?'

★   ★   ★

The lake was still now, with hardly a ripple on the surface of the water, and it was difficult to remember the violence of last night's storm, or how scared she had been. In the sunshine, with the trees full of early summer leaves, she felt safe, but another storm could blow up at any moment. Her life had been like that lately — never knowing when the next storm was going to blow all her carefully laid plans out of the water.

Where was her aunt?

From the moment she had locked the door of her flat behind her, she had been trying to contact Aunt Marjory.

She had risked an email as soon as she was told she would have to leave, and her aunt had replied immediately, telling her she was welcome anytime, but it had seemed only polite to say she was on her way and would need a place to stay until she found other accommodation.

The walk round the lake only took a slow half an hour, but by the time they reached the halfway mark Jake was already complaining. She couldn't afford to mollycoddle him and explained that children in other countries had to walk much further to get to school each day. She reasoned that if he could spend hours running around a playground or chasing pigeons in the park, he could cope with a leisurely stroll round a pretty lake. Maybe she should have given him the piggyback he was asking for, but there was no one to advise her right now. She swatted at something nasty buzzing round her head. There were flies in London, but the lake was swarming with a myriad of flying things she had never seen before, and most of them seemed to bite.

When they got back to the cabins, Theo was sitting outside with Rosie at his feet. 'Nice walk?'

She nodded to Theo and smiled when Jake suddenly got a new lease of life and ran up the steps to pet Rosie. 'He told me he was so tired he couldn't walk another step.'

Theo looked at the little boy. 'Straight to bed for you, then. Otherwise you might not have the energy to play with Rosie tomorrow.'

Jake looked sheepish for a moment, but then his face brightened. 'That's because we've stopped walking. I only get tired when I walk a long way.'

'But not when you run around?' Theo asked.

Jake shook his head. 'No. Only walking. I like running around.'

'That explains it, then.'

Sara laughed. 'He has his own set of values and they change all the time. You'll never keep up with him.'

'He'll make a good lawyer one day.'

But she had to get him registered at a school before he could become anything. He was supposed to start school in September, and she had no idea whether the infant school in the village where her aunt lived would be able to take him.

'I still can't contact my aunt,' she told Theo. 'I emailed her to tell her I was coming to see her, but not exactly when I would be arriving. I think I shall have to drive to Norfolk and hope I can find the village.'

'You don't have satnav in your car?'

She smiled. 'I probably do, but it's a rental and I have no idea how to set up the navigation system.'

'Remind me to do it for you before you leave.' He looked at her thoughtfully. 'I would like to invite you round to my cabin tonight because I still owe you a meal, but I know you can't leave Jake on his own. If it's OK I'll come to you again, only this time I'll order takeaway. Any preferences?'

It was on the tip of her tongue to refuse, but she would be leaving the cabin the next day and she didn't really want to spend her last evening alone. It was only for the evening, of course, and that was a pity, because a night with a tall, gorgeous man with eyes the colour of quicksilver was probably exactly what she needed. But nothing like that was going to happen anytime soon. Jake was the perfect chaperone.

'I didn't know you could get takeaway here. What do they have on offer?'

'Indian or pizza. No Chinese, I'm afraid. Wait — hang on a minute. I've got menus in my cabin.'

He was back in a couple of seconds with brightly coloured flyers and a pencil and paper. 'Write down what you want, and they'll deliver in about an hour. By the time Jake is bathed and in bed, it'll be ready to put on the table.' He grinned at her. 'I keep a stash of wine in case of unexpected guests, so you get to choose again. Red or white?'

She chose Indian rather than pizza, and they sorted out a set meal for two. The wine she left up to him. Back in the cabin, she put her grubby son in the shower and gave him a thorough wash while he held the shower head, giggling when he splashed her. By the time they were finished, she was nearly as wet as him. While she cooked him a supper of sausage and scrambled egg, she tried to work out what to wear. All her clothes had been stuffed into their one suitcase or somewhere in one of several carrier bags, and she couldn't wear the same jeans she had worn last night. Theo would think she didn't have any clothes. Thankful for the iron, she plugged it in while Jake devoured his food as if it was his last meal.

She hadn't told him they would be leaving, and intended putting that off until the very last minute. Just for once, she wanted him to be happy and not worried about where they were going next. And she wanted to enjoy her evening with Theo before she had to say goodbye. Perhaps, she thought, it would be best not to tell him. Just sneak away in the morning before he took Rosie for her walk. That would be a really cowardly thing to do, but right now it seemed the most sensible option.

The dress she chose didn't need much ironing. The fabric looked like silk, but was actually a synthetic that didn't crease. It had been one of her staples when she had to get Jake ready for nursery school before she left for work. It was silver-grey, which made her think again of Theo's mesmerising eyes, and in a simple style with a crossover bodice and a skirt cut on the bias. She thought it was quite demure, but one of the male researchers in her office had told her it was incredibly sexy. She had immediately stopped wearing it to work, but it was the only thing she had in her case that didn't look as if an elephant had trampled on it.

By the time she had read Jake a story, his eyes were already closing, and she congratulated herself for not giving him a piggyback. He had enjoyed a really busy day and, with a bit of luck, he should sleep like a baby.

She barely had time to brush her hair and smooth it into place with a squirt of spray when Theo knocked on her door. An enticing aroma of Indian spices followed him inside. He handed her a bottle of red wine and she smiled at him.

'I prefer red wine to white,' she said, 'but someone told me you should always drink white wine or beer with Indian food.'

'I don't do what I'm told, Sara. Not ever. You should make a note of that.' The grey eyes glinted. 'But red wine is fine if you watch out for the tannins.'

She had no idea what he was talking about. Her brain had gone into meltdown when he said he didn't do what he was told, but she nodded wisely. 'I'll try to remember to do that next time I'm faced with that particular dilemma.'

He laughed softly. 'Is Jake asleep?'

'Yes.'

'How do you know? Don't you need to look in the bedroom to make sure?'

She shook her head. 'If he was still awake he'd be in here right now, wanting to know what you're doing here.'

'What *am* I doing here, Sara?'

Her heart gave a little jump and she tried to ignore the flutter of excitement in the pit of her stomach. She didn't have the time or the energy for those sort of feelings. 'Bringing me food and wine, and intelligent conversation I hope, and, if I'm lucky . . . ' She let her voice tail off and looked into those hypnotic silver eyes. 'If I'm very lucky, I suppose you might help me with the washing up afterwards.'

'That might happen.' He twisted the top off the wine bottle and walked over to the table she had set earlier. 'But the key word is 'afterwards'.' He poured wine into both glasses and turned to look at her. 'After what? I wonder.'

Now was a good time to change the subject. 'I found out who Kevin

Spender is. At least I think I did.'

'He's a private investigator working for Spender Investigations, a Leeds-based privately owned company run by his father. At the moment they're at that difficult point where the company owes more than it has coming in.' He smiled at the look of astonishment on her face. 'I have a computer in my cabin, remember. I use it for my writing, and I have to do a lot of research, so I'm quite good at it.'

Sara took warm plates out of the oven, glad the subject had been changed. 'So how did he find me? I didn't know I was coming here. I turned off the main road because of the storm. If he'd followed me from London, he wouldn't be able to masquerade as a fisherman. He wouldn't have known this was a fisherman's retreat. I didn't.'

Theo opened the cartons and pulled out a chair for her. 'Let's eat before the food gets cold, then we'll have a discussion about Kevin Spender. My brain won't function on an empty stomach.'

Sara had made a bread-and-butter pudding with the bread and eggs in her welcome pack. She added a handful of dried fruit left over from her baked apples of the day before, and sprinkled sugar on top. She was quite pleased with the look of the golden-brown pudding when she took it out of the oven.

'How on earth did you manage to conjure up something like that when you haven't been shopping?'

She was ridiculously pleased at the look of admiration on his face. 'If you have a child to feed and not much money to spend, you get very good at improvisation. Be careful,' she told him hastily as he was about to pop a large spoonful in his mouth. 'The pudding is very hot.' She could still remember burning her tongue on her mother's bread-and-butter pudding when she was a child.

He washed the few items from dinner

while she made coffee. 'How did he find me, Theo?'

'I've been thinking about that. When do you plan on leaving here?'

'I was going to leave tomorrow,' she said warily. 'Why?'

'Can you stay another day? I want to take a good look at your car, and I need to do that in the daylight. When you were packing the car to leave, did you leave it outside your flat?'

'Yes,' she said. 'I had an allocated parking space but no car, so I picked up the rental the day before and left it outside all night.'

'So your car was left unattended until the next morning?'

'Yes,' she answered, puzzled. Then her mouth went dry. 'You don't think someone planted a bomb on my car, do you?'

He laughed, and her heartbeat returned to normal.

'What then?'

'Something almost as farfetched, but worth thinking about. I want to check for a tracking device. If you rule out the impossible, the improbable is most likely correct.'

'Kevin Spender was in the village yesterday,' she told Theo. 'Across the street from where we were parked. Jake recognised him this morning. I don't think he saw us. He was going into the bank.'

'It doesn't surprise you that someone might have put a tracker on your car?' When she didn't answer, he sighed. 'You don't have to tell me anything you don't want to, but I need a bit more information, Sara.'

It was her turn to sigh. 'I know.'

'If you want to keep it to yourself, fine, but I can't begin to help you unless I know what this is all about.'

She could see the exasperation in his eyes. She wanted to tell him, but she found it hard to bare her soul to a complete stranger. She hadn't told her secrets to anyone for a long time.

'Jake's grandfather wants to take Jake away from me. He's trying to make out

I'm not a fit mother so he can get full custody.'

6

Theo sat back in his chair. His eyes were bright with interest now, and she could almost see the cogs turning in his clever brain.

'I asked you this once before, Sara. What about Jake's father — what happened to him?'

'He's dead. That's what started this all off. After I graduated, my boyfriend, who was called Dominic, suggested we take a year out and go to America, and I agreed. I hadn't got over losing both my parents, and I suppose I was feeling needy.'

She looked down, not meeting Theo's eyes. She felt foolish and vulnerable. She knew she came across as a strong, independent woman, but most of the time she was shaking inside, trying to hold everything together because of Jake.

'Then what happened? Why do you think that Dominic's father is trying to take Jake away from you?'

'Because Dominic was an only son. He killed himself in one of his fast cars. I read about it in the paper. Of course I was sorry, Dominic was Jake's father, but I hadn't seen him for five years. I sent a sympathy card to Dominic's father. I didn't mention Jake but somehow he found out.'

Theo leant forward and put his elbows on the table, forcing her to look at him. 'He can't legally take your son away from you, Sara. I can make sure of that.'

She shook her head. 'You can't stop him. He's a millionaire — billionaire — I don't know. He's a millionaire several times over, and you can bet your life he's got the best lawyer money can buy.'

Theo leant back again, a smile on his lips. 'No, he hasn't. He hasn't got me.'

She managed a half-smile in return. 'You obviously weren't around when he was looking.'

'You said the grandfather was trying to make you look like a bad parent. What has he done, Sara? Whatever it is, it's probably illegal.'

She shook her head again. 'I don't think so. He's a very clever man. When I found out Dominic had died, I was managing pretty well. I had a job that paid really good money, a flat in London that I could just about afford, and my son was healthy and happy.' She laughed ruefully. 'What could possibly go wrong?'

Theo wanted to take her in his arms and soothe away the tension in her body, but now was not the time for sympathy. If he knew women as well as he thought he did, she would start crying and then fall apart, and he didn't want that to happen. He needed more information.

'What did go wrong?' he asked.

'I lost my job. I was accused of stealing. Not money, but information; and I was supposed to have passed it on to a competitor. I found out who the real culprit was, but I didn't have any proof. No one would stand up for me, so I was dismissed with a promise that if I went quietly no further action would be taken. I could have looked for another job, nothing was actually proved and I had my degree, but my landlord raised the rent on my flat yet again. I tried to get him to give me time to find somewhere else, but he wanted me out. Suddenly I had no job and nowhere to live.' She cleared her throat. 'So I phoned my Aunt Marjory and asked if we could stay with her for a couple of weeks and maybe look for somewhere to live near her. I couldn't afford London anymore, even if I got another job.'

'Don't you have any other relatives? Someone who could help you out?'

She laughed. 'Only the millionaire grandfather of my son.'

She was running away, and he couldn't blame her. With a good lawyer on her side, there was no way the grandfather would ever get custody; but

Theo knew first-hand how stressful a court case could be, particularly if the custody of a child was involved. She was homeless, without a job, and pretty desperate. Without saying anything, he refilled her glass with wine and waited for her to continue.

'First of all, I got a letter from a lawyer informing me Dominic's father would be asking for custody of his grandchild. The letter was in legal jargon, but it suggested I was not in the best position, emotionally or financially, to bring up a four-year-old child. I was told there would be free accommodation for me and my child, and money would be provided for Jake to go to a recognised private school of my choosing. It was made to sound as if it would be wicked of me to deprive Jake of an opportunity like that.' She sighed. 'I was so desperate, for a while I even considered it.'

'What made you change your mind?'

She managed a grin this time. 'I suddenly remembered what a prat

Dominic had turned out to be. But when I refused the offer, the lawyer told me Mr Cassidy would be taking the matter further because he believed his grandson's future was in jeopardy. After that, every time there was a knock on the door I thought someone had come to take Jake away. I managed to get packed and move out of London within a week.'

She yawned, and he got to his feet. 'You're tired, Sara. Sorry for the cross-examination, but you won't have to do it again, I promise. This will never go to court. What did you say the grandfather's name was?'

'Milton Cassidy.'

'Of Cassidy Leisure centres?'

'Yes. He has places everywhere.' She frowned. 'Why do rich people have such odd first names, like Dominic and Milton?'

Theo laughed. 'Probably because they're prats. Stop worrying and get some sleep. I'll look at the car tomorrow out of sight of our fisherman

110

friend. I can't think of any other way he could have found you. From what you say, he's probably being paid a small fortune to keep you in sight. Although I would have thought someone like Cassidy would have employed a more reputable company.'

She was right behind him when he got to the door, and when he turned to look at her she put her hand on his arm. 'Thank you. I normally cope better than this, but I really thought I was getting us both away from that man. I never dreamed he would have us followed.'

'Why is it so important for him to have custody of his grandson?'

'Dominic told me his father was going to leave him everything, including the company. The business has belonged to the Cassidy's for generations, but Dominic was the last of the line. Now Milton needs an heir. He'll groom my son to take over the family business.'

Theo opened the door, but then Theo hesitated before he stepped out into the night. He could have talked her into letting him stay. That was what he was good at. He considered it for a couple of minutes and then stifled a frustrated sigh. Sometimes he wished he didn't have such an irritating sense of honour.

'That won't happen, Sara. Not unless you want it to.'

She stood beside him, looking out at the dark water of the lake. 'Should I want it to? Would it be better for Jake if I let it happen?'

He turned round and took her by the shoulders, kicking the door shut. He wanted to shake her. He could see by the look in her eyes that she no longer trusted herself to make the right choice for her son. But instead of shaking her, he pulled her into his arms and kissed her. She didn't push him away, but she didn't kiss him back either. She was passive, her lips soft under his. Reluctantly, because his body was telling him to do the opposite, he released her.

She stepped back and looked into his eyes, a small frown on her face. 'Did you kiss me because you feel sorry for me? I'm grateful for your help, Theo, but I don't need your sympathy. I may fall down a few times, but I always manage to pick myself up. And in answer to your question, no, I don't think it would be better for Jake to live with his grandfather. But he's not old enough to make that sort of decision, and I don't want him to hate me later on for standing in his way.'

'So you have to trust yourself to make that decision for him. There must have been a lot of times already when you weren't sure if you were doing the right thing, but you went ahead anyway.' He pulled her into his arms again. 'Like right now. There doesn't always have to be a reason. Sometimes we do what feels right at the time. And, unless you've lost all sense of feeling, you must realise sympathy has no part in why I want to kiss you.'

This time she did kiss him back, but when his fingers found the zipper on the back of her dress she moved away from him again. 'Jake's in the next room, Theo, and sometimes he wakes up and comes looking for me.'

'I'm sorry. I wasn't thinking.' Which was a big fat lie, but the idea of Jake walking in on what he *had* been thinking acted like a cold shower. He pulled the door open again and stepped outside. 'I was right, wasn't I? You've proved you can trust yourself to make the right decision.' He turned back before she closed the door and gave her a quick kiss on the lips. 'There will be a time when we can carry on where we left off without fear of interruption, and I can wait if you can. Now get some sleep. I'll see you tomorrow.'

He saw her smile, and closed the door before he could change his mind. Barricading Jake in his room would work, wouldn't it? How did people with a house full of assorted kids manage?

There had to be a way, otherwise couples would only have one child.

Once he was back in his cabin, he poured himself a shot of whisky. There was definitely a gap in the market for a child warning system. He thought of everything from bells sown on to their pyjamas to a laser beam across the bedroom doorway. His best idea, he decided, was a chip implanted in a child at birth that could tell exactly where they were at any given moment. A parent would be able to track their child on a mobile phone.

He fell asleep thinking of a draconian state where everyone had a tracking device fitted by law.

★ ★ ★

Sara woke to the sound of birds. It was more usual to find Jake standing beside her asking for his breakfast, and she realised this must be because he had spent most of the previous day outdoors. Not so long ago she had dreaded the idea of moving to the country. She loved the bustle of the city; the fact that everything she wanted was on her doorstep. She loved the noise and the excitement, the red buses and black taxi cabs, the theatres and designer shops; but now she was beginning to realise rural life wasn't only creepy-crawlies and scary cows. It had amazing sunsets and stars you could actually see at night.

She had showered and dressed and was on her second cup of coffee before her son wandered into the room, rubbing a hand over his eyes. 'Is it morning yet?'

'Yes. You slept in. The birds are singing and the lake looks fantastic. A couple of swans arrived in the night and they look as if they're here to stay.'

'Perhaps they had to leave their home like we did,' Jake said.

She put her coffee mug down. 'Did you mind very much? You had to leave all your friends behind, didn't you? I'm sorry.'

'I don't mind. I like our holiday. Can I have breakfast now? Toast and jam and milk, please.'

She busied herself making toast for both of them. She wanted to tell him they were going to leave for Norfolk today, but she hadn't the heart. Let him have his breakfast first, and she would have one more go at contacting Aunt Marjory.

When she eventually opened the door so Jake could go outside, she found Theo leaning on her car in conversation with Kevin Spender. He looked up when she appeared on the veranda.

'Hi, Sara. I've had a look at your car but I can't find anything likely to be making the noise you were worried about. Kevin knows a bit about cars and he can't find anything wrong, either.'

Sara realised Theo had probably been caught in the act of crawling round under her car and had made up a story about a mysterious noise.

'It was one of those intermittent things. You know, the thing garage mechanics hate the most.' She gave Kevin an innocent look. 'I'll be leaving soon, and it's a long drive to King's Lynn.'

'It certainly is. You wandered a bit off track if you came straight from London.'

'Yes, I know. I thought the back roads would be less busy, but then I got lost in the storm and took a wrong turning. I was lucky to find this place in the dark.' She smiled at him sweetly. 'How did you know we came from London? Was it my accent?'

He was good; she had to give him that. There was a look in his eyes, just for a second, which told her he was cursing himself for his mistake, but he recovered quickly.

'Lack of one, actually. East Anglia has a mix of accents, but most of them are quite distinct. You'll notice it when you get up into the wilds of Norfolk. Another holiday, or will you be staying there for good?'

King's Lynn was hardly the wilds of Norfolk, but the man was fishing for information.

'Not sure yet,' she told him, adding a little shrug for good measure. 'We'll be renting for a bit to see how we like it. I need to get Jake into a school by September, so I need to find a good one, but there's no immediate hurry.'

'The car seems fine,' Theo said. 'Are you planning on leaving today?'

She frowned. Was she supposed to answer yes or no to that? 'No,' she said after a moment's hesitation. 'Now the weather has taken a turn for the better, I think I'll stay a couple more days. Jake loves it here, and like I said, there's no hurry to get where we're going.'

'Great,' Theo said, beaming at her. 'I'll see you later, then.'

Yes, you will, she thought crossly. She would ask for a script next time so she didn't have to ad-lib; but judging by his smile, she'd evidently said the right things. She left Jake with strict instructions not to go out of sight of the cabin and went back inside to wash up their breakfast dishes. She wasn't surprised when Theo knocked on her door half an hour later.

'What was that all about? I didn't know what you wanted me to say.'

'I didn't want you to tell Spender you were leaving today. He'd be after you like a shot. Follow you all the way to the wilds of Norfolk if needs be.'

'I'm not going to King's Lynn. My aunt lives near Norwich.'

'Quite a way from King's Lynn, then. Good for you. If Spender tries to get ahead of you, he'll be heading in the wrong direction.'

'What about my car? Did you find anything?'

Theo shook his head. 'No, but Spender came out before I could do a proper search. Besides, I don't think I'd find a tracking device even if there was one. They make them so small these days, and Spender is a professional. He won't have put it anywhere obvious.

But I can't think of any other way he could have found you.'

She looked at him helplessly. She was up against a millionaire and a professional investigator. She might have The Ice Man on her side, but he wouldn't come into his own unless she faced Milton Cassidy in court. And that wasn't going to happen, so once she left Dante's Lake she'd be on her own again.

'So what do I do now?'

He sat on her sofa and reached for her hand so he could pull her down beside him. 'I've thought of a plan. We'll leave your car here and I'll drive you and Jake to your aunt's.'

She started to protest. She owed Theo enough already, and she had a nasty feeling she was beginning to rely on him. She had to be independent, otherwise leaving London would be a wasted effort. She'd made too many compromises already. It wasn't only Theo who had a plan. She had been planning this trip for weeks, and if the storm hadn't blown them off course she would already be with her aunt.

'I can't let you do that,' she said firmly. 'I need to do this on my own, and I've thought of something I can do that might help slow him down. If I let Mr Spender's tyres down before I leave, he won't be able to follow me until it's too late. I'll get a map so I won't get lost again, and I won't be going in the direction Spender thinks I am.' She felt pleased with herself. The more she thought about it, the better the plan seemed. It couldn't really fail.

'How are you planning on letting his tyres down?'

'Unscrew some thingy on the tyres? Or poke holes in them, maybe.'

'It's not that easy, Sara. You don't just turn a knob and all the air comes out. You need to know what you're doing.'

She had thought it was quite a good idea, but obviously not. She got up and walked over to the sink to fill the kettle. At least she could make a cup of tea. Boiling water didn't involve a great deal of technical knowledge. She looked out of the window but Jake was nowhere in sight.

'I can't see Jake. Or Rosie. Did you leave her with him when you came in here?'

'Yes.' Theo got up and came to stand beside her. 'She would have barked if Jake got into any sort of trouble. I told her to watch him.'

Sara opened the door and stepped outside. There was no sign of Jake, and she felt her heart rate start to pick up. Theo joined her and called to his dog. At first there was nothing, but then a bark echoed across the water.

The little boat was right in the centre of the lake. She could see Rosie standing up, her front feet on the side of the boat, but it looked as if Jake was sitting down. Theo came up beside her and grabbed her arm before she could shout to her son.

'If he stands up, he might tip the boat over. At the moment he's fine. All we have to do is keep him that way until I can get to him.'

'How are you going to do that?'

She felt panic clutch at her heart and make it beat fast enough to shake her whole body, and with the panic was a terrible sense of guilt. She had meant to take Jake swimming and to book him a few lessons at the local pool. But she was working during the week and there was always something more important to do at the weekend, so he had never learned, and now he was going to drown because of her laziness.

'He can't swim,' she said.

'Well then, let's hope he won't have to.' Theo pulled his shirt over his head and bent down to take off his shoes, but then he stood up again. 'What's he doing?'

Sara squinted across the water. She saw Jake reach down and then throw something over the side of the boat into the lake. When he did it again, her heart almost stopped beating. She looked at Theo.

'He's bailing water out of the boat.'

Theo finished undoing his shoes and started unzipping his jeans. 'That's why Jake hasn't spotted us yet. He's too busy bailing out water. Rosie knows she has to guard Jake, so she'll stay in the boat with him.'

'How long will it be before the boat sinks?'

He turned to look at her as he kicked off his jeans and, just for one tiny moment, she almost forgot her son was stranded in a sinking boat in the middle of the lake. There was a streak of dark hair running down the middle of Theo's chest that disappeared below the top of his close-fitting underpants. His body was toned like an athlete's. The only thing marring absolute perfection was the scar on his thigh where the bullet had been removed.

'There was a storm the other night, remember. The boat isn't leaking; it's got rain water in the bottom.' He patted her arm. 'Don't worry, the boat won't sink, and I promise I'll get to him before he falls in the water.'

With that, he was gone. She watched him walk into the lake until the water was up to his waist, and then start out towards the boat with an overarm stroke that looked easy. When he was halfway to the boat, Rosie saw him and started barking — and Jake stood up. Sara felt lightheaded with fear as she watched the little boat start to rock. Jake tried to keep his feet, but in the end he gave up and sat down again. She heard Theo shout something, and Rosie sat as well. After a couple of seconds, the boat stopped rocking and Sara took a breath.

It only took Theo another few minutes to reach the boat and carefully haul himself on board. She saw him talking to Jake and patting Rosie to calm her down, and then he pushed a couple of oars over the side and into the water.

Once the boat started moving, Theo used long strokes on the oars until he was close enough to get out and use the rope to pull the little boat on to the shingle. He lifted Jake over the side with Rosie close behind, and then he leant forward with his hands on his bent knees, getting his breath back.

Sara grabbed Jake in a hug that had him wriggling to get away. He looked none the worse for all the excitement and he was fairly dry, apart from the bottom of his shorts. Theo, on the other hand, looked absolutely done in. Reserving the tongue-lashing she would have given Jake had she been on her own, she sent him inside to get towels. Theo had looked pretty good when he first stripped off and stood before her clad only in his snug underpants; but walking out of the water pulling a boat behind him, he beat Mr Darcy hands down.

When Jake came back carrying a couple of towels, she threw one to Theo while she wrapped Jake in the other. She really needed to get the man covered up before she made a fool of herself.

Jake looked at Theo in awe. 'He's a

hero, isn't he, Mummy? He saved my life.'

Sara thought that might have been a bit melodramatic, but she nodded in agreement. It would be a couple more minutes before she could trust herself to speak.

7

Theo took the towel gratefully. He was finding it difficult to look like a hero when he couldn't get his breath, and even more difficult to live up to the image after being immersed in cold water. The rowing had made him sweat, but his nether regions were still wet and cold. He wrapped the towel round his waist and pulled the boat further up the little beach, making sure it couldn't slip back into the water.

'Spender had his door open,' Sara said. 'I saw him shut it when we both came outside. I expect he was taking pictures, more ammunition for Milton Cassidy if it comes to a court case. Leaving my son in the middle of a lake alone in a boat while I entertain a man in my cabin is definitely not something a caring mother would do.'

He hated seeing her looking so

defenceless, but most women would have given up already. He held up the rope so Sara could see it. 'The boat wasn't tied up.'

'So if Jake was playing in the boat, it could easily have drifted out into the middle of the lake by itself.'

That wasn't quite the scenario Theo had envisaged, but he didn't want to upset Sara any more than necessary; she'd had enough worry for one day. Admittedly the rope had only been loosely tied to the post the last time he'd walked past the boat, but he was sure Spender had something to do with the boat being in the middle of the lake.

'I need to shower and change. Get Jake inside and keep him warm; I'll be round in a few minutes.' He looked at Jake, now playing happily with Rosie. The child didn't look the slightest bit traumatised. Most children were incredibly resilient; he saw that every day. Whether they had to cope with a marital break-up or a parent going to prison, most of them came out of it relatively unscathed. What counted was the love and support they received after the event.

He hoped Sara wouldn't question her son until later. At the moment the little boy was expecting to get told off by his mother and would say anything that would get him out of trouble. Theo had questioned children in court — not as young as Jake, maybe — but he knew how to put them at ease. It was part of his job. Within ten minutes he was knocking on Sara's door. She opened it with a smile on her face.

'I didn't get a chance to thank you. Swimming out to that boat and then rowing it back to shore was amazing. You probably really did save Jake's life.'

'I doubt it; he was doing fine on his own. He didn't panic, he just got on with the job of bailing out the boat.' He sat down next to Jake, who was sitting on the sofa eating a cupcake. 'Hi, Jake. Have you told your mother how you came to get stranded out there on the lake?'

Sara shook her head. 'Not yet. I thought I'd give him time to warm up and have something to eat.'

'So how did it happen?' Theo asked. 'Was the boat tied up when you got in it?'

'I don't know. I didn't look. Rosie got in as well, and we were playing *Pirates of the Caribbean*.'

When Sara started to say something, Theo held up his hand. 'Then what happened?' He wanted to make sure she didn't accuse Jake of anything. He shouldn't have been playing in the boat because his mother had told him not to, but he wasn't quite five yet and Theo would have been even more worried if the child did everything he was told.

'I pretended I was a pirate, and we were jumping about in the boat. The Mr Spender man came and asked where my mummy was because the boat was in the water. Rosie growled because she doesn't like him, and he went away.' He looked at his mother reproachfully. 'I shouted, but you didn't come. Rosie wanted to get out, but I told her to stay in the boat in case she drowned. There was water in the bottom, so I got handfuls and threw it out.'

'That was very clever of you,' Theo said admiringly. 'Did Mr Spender, the fisherman who was hiding in the bushes, untie the rope?'

'I don't know. I think it came untied by itself.' He looked at his mother. 'I'm sorry, Mummy. Me and Rosie were only playing.'

'I know you were. But if you hadn't got in the boat, you wouldn't have finished up in the middle of the lake, would you?'

Jake looked crestfallen. 'I won't do it again.'

Theo got to his feet. He had managed to hold on to his temper this long because he didn't want to upset Sara or Jake, but Spender had just left that boat to float away. He was responsible for putting the life of a four-year-old in danger, and it could very easily have turned into a tragedy.

'I won't be long,' he told Sara, 'but I need to talk to that man.'

She put a hand on his arm. 'Be careful, Theo. I don't want to be accused of aiding and abetting in a case of GBH.'

'If it comes to blows,' Theo told her, 'I promise you mine won't show. You learn a lot being a defence lawyer.' But he didn't intend getting into a scrap with the likes of Spender. The man wasn't worth the effort.

He walked the few yards to Spender's cabin and knocked on the door, pleased to see a flicker of fear in the man's eyes when he saw who was waiting outside.

'We need to talk.' He shook his head when Spender attempted to step outside. 'No, inside. I'm not carrying on a conversation on your doorstep.' He pushed past Spender before the man had a chance to stop him, and walked inside.

The place looked neat and tidy, with nothing lying about. Spender had been living out of his suitcase, ready to make a quick getaway if he needed to. Ready, Theo thought, to follow Sara and Jake as soon as they left.

He was pretty sure about the tracking device, but the man in front of him was a professional and he wouldn't have put a tracker anywhere obvious.

'The child says you left him to drift out into the middle of the lake. He's only a little kid. He could have drowned.'

Spender shook his head. 'A kid will say anything to get out of trouble. Besides, that's not what happened. I wouldn't do something like that. The kid was jumping around and the rope had come loose. I'm surprised his mother wasn't nearby keeping an eye on him.'

'So you just let the boy and the dog float away in front of you? You could have pulled the boat back onto the shore before it got too far out.'

Spender shrugged. 'I started to, but that dog of yours was growling at me. I wasn't going to hang around and get bitten. The dog and the kid, they're not my responsibility. Maybe the kid's mother should do more to keep him safe. You think a lot of that boy, don't you? And the woman.' He gave a sly grin. 'You wouldn't want to lose either of them, would you?'

Theo closed his eyes for a second. He really didn't want to start a fight with the man, but he found his hands were already clenched into fists. He breathed out and counted to ten, and then he walked over to the camera sitting on the table and picked it up.

'Is this your camera?'

'What of it?'

Still keeping an eye on Spender, Theo carefully opened the camera and took out the memory card. 'I'll keep this, if you don't mind. Taking pictures of a child without consent is illegal.'

Spender shrugged. 'Not a problem; I always keep a spare copy. But I wasn't taking pictures of the boy. I wouldn't do anything illegal.'

Theo put the card in his pocket and studied the camera. 'I don't want you to do anything illegal, either, so I'll make sure you can't take any more pictures you're not supposed to.'

Theo picked up the camera and carried it to the sink, turning on the tap before Spender could stop him.

'That camera's worth a couple of thousand quid! What the hell's the matter with you? Just 'cause you're a lawyer, I suppose you think you can get away with something like that, but you won't. I'll bloody well sue you, you see if I don't.'

'Trouble is,' Theo said sadly, 'you need evidence to sue anyone, and you weren't taking any pictures of me drowning your camera, were you?'

He put the dripping camera back on the table and let himself out. Ruining the camera had been petty and unnecessary, but it had made him feel a whole lot better. Spender might have a copy of his photos, but the memory card would show exactly what those photos were, and taking photos of a little kid was a risky business.

He walked back to Sara's cabin and knocked on her door. She opened the door and stood looking at him, then she took hold of his right hand and examined his knuckles.

'No fisticuffs, then.'

Theo smiled at her as he walked past her into the cabin. 'No fisticuffs, but I got the memory card from his camera.' He held it out so she could see it. 'Then his camera got broken somehow.'

'I bet he wasn't happy about that.' She frowned. 'So what happened? Spender let you take the card and break his camera and didn't do anything about it?'

Theo had a feeling Sara had been worried about him, and that gave him a warm glow. 'He wasn't exactly happy, but he says he has a copy of the photos, which makes sense — and he's going to sue me. I'm not sure what for. Probably malicious damage, or maybe for looking at him in a threatening manner. You needn't have worried; I knew he wouldn't start a fight. I'm bigger than him.'

'I wasn't worried about him starting a fight. I was worried about you starting a fight. You looked pretty aggressive when you left here.'

Theo glanced at Jake, who was sitting on the sofa wrapped in a duvet. He didn't want the little boy to be frightened of him. 'Not aggressive at all. I wanted to have a word with Mr Spender, that's all.'

Theo had thought Jake was too interested in the game on his tablet to be listening, but now he looked up. 'Rosie doesn't like Mr Spender. She made a noise at him and you could see her teeth. Mr Spender thought Rosie was going to bite him.'

'But she didn't bite him.' Theo didn't want Jake to be scared of Rosie, either. 'She has never bitten anyone, and she loves you, Jake. That's why she looks after you.'

'I know. I love her, too.' He looked at his mother. 'I'm hungry.'

'Lunch will have to be cheese on toast then, because that's all I've got.'

Theo knew that was his cue to go, but he didn't want to leave Sara alone. She still looked a little shaky, even though she was good at covering up her feelings. He wanted to take her in his arms and tell her everything was going to be all right, but Jake was watching his every move. The little boy appeared to enjoy having a man around, but Theo knew it would only take one false move. Even at such a young age, Jake was intensely protective of his mother, and Theo thought it was a credit to Sara that he was so well adjusted and well behaved. From what Sara said, Jake had never had a man in his life. She had been too busy working and bringing up her son to get involved in any serious relationships.

'Can I stay for lunch?' he asked.

Sara raised an eyebrow. 'Cheese on toast? Really, Theo? You may be used to Croque Monsieur at a classy restaurant, but my cheese on toast is just that. No slices of juicy ham included.'

'I don't like ham,' Jake said.

'Well, that's settled then.' Theo dropped the memory card back into his pocket. 'Plain cheese on toast, the way granny used to make it.'

'Do you have a granny?' Jake asked curiously. 'I don't. My granny died, but my friend has *three* grannies.'

He said it as if the distribution of grannies should be better organised. And, when Theo thought about it, it did seem a little unfair. Perhaps all the grannies should be put in a big bag and allocated more evenly, so every child got at least one.

'Your granny would have been very proud of you this morning,' Sara said with a smile. 'You were very brave. I want you to eat your lunch slowly, and then you can have a little rest. Maybe we'll go for a walk round the lake later on and take Rosie with us, but only if you have a rest first.'

Theo hoped he was invited to the walk round the lake. He found he liked being included in Sara's plans. What had started out as a tedious few weeks getting over a bullet wound had turned into something much more interesting.

Once Jake was settled in the bedroom with the door closed, Theo made coffee and Sara sat beside him on the sofa. 'This is all a bit too cosy,' she said worriedly. 'I don't want Jake to think this is the way it's always going to be. We'll be driving up to stay with my aunt in Norfolk, and you have to get back to your work. This is all going to end very soon, and I'm afraid Jake will be really upset. There's no way I can avoid that.' She held up her hand when he tried to interrupt. 'I can't let this happen, Theo. It's not fair to any of us.'

She was looking down, staring into her coffee cup, and he put his finger under her chin and tilted it up. 'Can't let what happen, Sara?' he asked softly.

He tried to keep his voice steady but it came out a little shaky.

She faced him squarely, her brown eyes sad. 'This. Us. Whatever it is that's happening. I can't get involved with you, Theo, even if I want to.'

He felt his heart rate increase and his palms start to sweat. Right this minute The Ice Man was in danger of melting. How could he face a courtroom full of people without showing any emotion, and then go to pieces in front of a pretty woman? He knew if he spoke he was going to stutter, so he took her hand instead — and watched her eyes fill with tears.

That was his undoing.

He pulled her roughly into his arms and held her while she sobbed into his shoulder. His own eyes were wet, and he fervently hoped Jake didn't suddenly appear from the bedroom. His macho image would be in ruins. After a couple of minutes, Sara lifted her head and brushed a hand across her face.

'Sorry. This isn't like me. I don't cry. Not usually. I think Jake getting stuck on the lake was the last straw. It's been a bit of a rollercoaster lately, but that's no excuse.' She untangled herself from his arms. 'You should go, Theo. Back to your own cabin. You're supposed to be recuperating. The last thing you need is a neurotic woman crying all over you.'

'You're hardly neurotic, Sara. You're one of the bravest women I've ever met.'

'If you make me cry again, I'll really hate you.' She took a deep breath. 'In spite of everything, I still have a life to lead. I have a plan, a road to follow, and I can't change everything mid-stream.'

'You can't change your plans just because you met me. I understand that.' Although he didn't, not all of it. Plans were meant to be changed because life changed. There was always something new waiting round the next corner. Sara had fallen into the trap of tunnel vision — refusing to see anything except the path she had plotted out for herself — and he did understand that. She had managed to plan a route through the chaos that surrounded her, and now she was scared of veering off course.

He decided it was best to agree with her. For the moment, anyway. 'So when are you leaving?'

She looked puzzled, obviously expecting an argument and slightly disappointed because she hadn't got one. 'Tomorrow morning. I'm sure you scared Spender off — and what can he do, anyway? He already has pictures of me behaving like the worst mother in the world. If Dominic's father tries to take Jake away from me, I'll give you a call. I might need you then.'

But she didn't need him now. He hoped he could change that. He had a vision of Spender stopping her on a dark, lonely road in that clapped-out car of his. He knew it was highly unlikely that would actually happen, as Spender was a paid investigator, not a psycho. He had probably intended taking a picture of Jake a few feet out in the lake while he held the rope, but unfortunately Rosie had other ideas. Spender was scared of the dog and dropped the rope, letting the boat drift out of reach.

It didn't really matter what actually happened, because if Sara left, Spender would follow her.

'I have a better idea,' he said. 'We have to stop Spender following you to your aunt's house.'

'And how are we going to do that? If he put a bug on my car, he's going to be able to track us whatever we do.'

'Not if we go in my car.'

She hesitated, her brow furrowed while she thought it through. 'But if he sees us leave, even if we go in your car, he'll still follow us.'

Theo grinned at her. 'I've thought about that, and I have a solution that might work.'

8

She had a problem with Jake the next morning. He didn't want to leave and refused to get dressed. She didn't want to carry him kicking and screaming out to the car because that would mess up all their carefully laid plans. She knew if she told him Theo and Rosie were going with them, Jake would happily leave the cabin, but she was worried he would blurt it all out to Spender.

'We're only going to the shop in the village,' she told him. 'That's all. And then we'll meet Theo and Rosie later.'

'Where are our cases?'

She sighed. Sometimes she wished her son wasn't quite so bright. 'They're somewhere safe so we can't forget them, OK?'

He nodded reluctantly and followed her outside to the car.

For a moment she didn't think

Spender was going to make an appearance, but she made a show of banging the car doors and opening the boot a couple of times and he appeared on his veranda. She pushed up the boot lid again so he could see it was empty.

'Are you leaving, Miss Finch?' Spender asked politely. 'I'll be sorry to see you go, and I hope you don't think badly of me. Your boyfriend seems to think I let your son drift out onto the lake, but he was quite mistaken.'

'I'm sure he was,' Sara said equally politely. 'But he's not my boyfriend, not like you mean. We're just friends.'

'I'm sorry if I misunderstood.' Spender gave her a knowing smile and came down his steps so he could see into her car. 'Can I help you carry out your cases?'

'Oh, we're not leaving yet. I thought I'd left a water bottle in the car somewhere, but I can't find it, so I'm going to drive into the village and get another one. I can't do that long drive without a bottle of water, and I need to get something for us to eat on the journey; probably a couple of packets of sandwiches.'

She was about to bundle Jake into the car when Spender spoke to him. 'You're leaving today then, son?'

'No, not yet. We're going to the village.'

Sara felt like giving Jake a hug. He had said exactly the right thing without being prompted. She strapped him into his seat and turned to Spender.

'I'll see you before we go, Mr Spender, and I might take you up on that offer to carry our cases outside.'

As she drove away, she looked in her rear-view mirror. Spender was still standing on his veranda watching them. She turned the corner past the last cabin and breathed a sigh of relief. She hoped Jake would be warm enough. He was only wearing short trousers and a T-shirt, but he could always change later if the weather deteriorated. She drove her car into the village and parked in a corner of the general car park, getting a two-hour ticket from the machine. Then she took Jake's hand and they walked to the Rose and Crown.

'We're going to have breakfast in the hotel and then wait for Theo and Rosie.'

'I thought we were going back to the cabin,' Jake said, frowning at her. 'I want my tablet — and Bugsy.'

They grow up too quickly, Sara thought sadly. A year ago Bugsy would have been first on the list.

'Theo is bringing everything with him. He has our cases and your tablet in his car. Rosie is looking after Bugsy until they get here, OK?'

Jake nodded happily as Sara led him to a table. She ordered two lots of scrambled eggs on toast and coffee for herself. Jake asked for a chocolate milkshake but she told him he had to eat his eggs first.

Theo had assured her that even if Spender drove to the village and found her parked car, he wouldn't think to look for them at the hotel. She hoped he was right. She managed to keep Jake amused for an hour, which was a first. He ate his breakfast far too quickly and she had to take him into the lounge area and play I-spy with him, followed by a game of alphabet animals which entailed trying to think of an animal that began with each letter of the alphabet starting with A. She breathed a sigh of relief when Theo walked in with Rosie on her lead.

'No problem?'

She shook her head. 'Spender came outside right on cue and got a good look at the inside of my car. He even offered to help with our cases when I get back.'

Jake was fussing with Rosie and trying to ask twenty questions at once.

'Please, Jake,' she said, 'if you wait a minute I'll explain.' She pulled a face at Theo. 'He won't shut up until I explain.' She didn't want to lie to her son, but she didn't want him to know that Spender had been hunting them down. 'Our car doesn't belong to us, it's rented, so we're going to leave it here in the village for the garage to pick up and Theo is going to drive us to Aunty Marjory's house.'

He beamed with delight and then frowned. 'But I need my tablet. I've just started a new game.'

'Don't worry,' Theo told him. 'It's in my car. So is your rabbit.' He turned to Sara. 'We need to go. There's a very small chance Spender might drive to the village looking for you. I know he didn't follow me because his car was still outside his cabin when I left.'

She got to her feet. 'We'll have to stop by my car and pick up Jake's car seat.'

He shook his head. 'Already done. I found your car, and where you'd hidden the keys, and swapped it over before I came here.'

They got Jake settled in the back of the big car with his tablet and stuffed rabbit, and Sara slid in beside Theo. She felt nervous and excited all at the same time. Now she really was on her way to her new life. She realised she felt a lot safer with The Ice Man sitting beside her. He must have felt her eyes on him, because he turned his head to glance at her, giving her a reassuring smile. How had he got that nickname? she wondered. His smile was warm enough to make her heart beat a little faster and bring a flush of heat to her cheeks.

Stop it! she told herself sternly. *He's just being kind, nothing else.* And she was right off men, anyway.

After about an hour Jake said he needed the toilet, and Theo suggested they leave the road they were on and make a diversion through a couple of villages.

'It will give me a chance to check Spender isn't following us, and the satnav will keep us going in the right direction. There's bound to be a coffee shop or a pub in one of the villages.'

When he pulled into a small parking area outside a pub called The Norfolk

Punch, she was glad to get out and stretch her legs. Rosie needed a pit stop too, and Sara was sure the little dog gave a thankful sigh as she relieved herself on a patch of grass.

Sara knew some pubs didn't open until midday, but the door to the lounge bar stood half open, and when they trooped inside they were greeted with a cheerful smile from the lady behind the bar. Her hair was a mix of grey and brown, and she had hazel eyes that picked up the brown of her sweater. She came round the bar to pet Rosie and told Theo it was perfectly all right for Rosie to remain inside.

'We have a separate eating area and dogs aren't allowed in there, but here in the bar area it's fine.'

Sara ordered coffee and Theo told the woman he'd love a pint, but as he was driving he'd stick with coffee as well. Jake wanted another milkshake, but Sara didn't want to risk him throwing up on Theo's leather upholstery, so she suggested a very small scoop of ice cream. She hoped that would keep him going until they either stopped for lunch or reached her aunt's village. She noticed Theo had placed his chair so he could see out of the window.

'Do you still think he might find us?' she asked.

'No,' he said immediately, and then shrugged. 'I don't think so. I don't see how he could. There would have been no reason to put a tracker on my car, and I don't think he'd want to take the chance of me finding it. If he did, and I found it, I would make sure he lost his job and never got another one. Not in that line of business, anyway.'

'But he'd get away with putting a bug on my car? Why Theo? I haven't done anything wrong. Not anything he could prove.'

Theo reached across the table and put his hand over hers. 'I know you haven't, but you're his assignment. He was sent out to find you and check your movements, so he's not responsible, his boss is.'

'Jake's grandfather,' she said bitterly. Jake was kneeling on a window seat watching the ducks on the pond in the middle of the village green and wasn't paying any attention to their conversation, but she kept her voice down. 'I don't understand how he can be so vindictive.'

Theo also glanced at Jake before he answered. 'I know there are no excuses for his behaviour. But he's just lost his only son, and Jake is his grandson, possibly the only family he has left. He probably thought you'd jump at the chance to live with him. Why wouldn't you? It would be easy enough for him to find out you'd lost your job and needed somewhere to live. He might have thought he was doing you a favour.'

Sara looked at him in amazement. She'd thought he understood, but he obviously didn't understand any of it. 'By setting an investigator on me? Getting someone to take photos that make me look as if I'm not fit to look after my own son?' She shook her head in disbelief. 'Do you think I'm a bad mother as well, not able to look after Jake?'

'He's been taking pictures of me as well. Maybe he's a mad photographer on a fishing trip.'

Jake had sensed something was wrong and turned from the window, looking at his mother worriedly. She had to stop being paranoid, she told herself, which was quite difficult when someone was following you. Theo put his hand over hers again and she almost pulled away, but instead she closed her eyes for a second and took a deep breath.

'Sorry,' she told him. 'I know I'm oversensitive where Jake's concerned, but he's all I've got.' She smiled at her son to let him know she was fine. 'You're right, of course, and I'd like Jake to meet his grandfather one day, but I don't know the man. I have no idea what he's really like.'

'Exactly,' Theo said, his hand still

covering hers. 'Perhaps I could set up a meeting. If you meet Cassidy with your lawyer present, he can't intimidate you.'

She sighed. 'I've let myself become paranoid, haven't I? It was all too much all at once. I could have coped with Milton Cassidy if my life had been settled, but losing my job and then my flat, and then him suggesting I couldn't bring up Jake on my own — that nearly pushed me over the edge. We'd been doing fine, and then suddenly my world got turned upside down. I was homeless and jobless and I couldn't see any way out. I know I could have got help, but it would have taken time, and I only had four weeks before I was out on the street. No one could have organised a home for us in that time. It would have been a shelter of some sort, and I couldn't bear the thought of that, not when I'd been managing so well. It all seemed so unfair.'

'It *is* unfair.' He gave her hand a squeeze and then let it go. 'Thank God for Aunt Marjory. You've got a new start ahead of you.' He looked at his watch. 'We'd better move if we want to get there in daylight, and we may need to stop for something to eat.'

'Jake has had quite enough to keep him going until teatime, and we might be there by then.' Feeling better, she took her phone out of her bag and looked at the screen. 'I'll try my aunt again when we get nearer civilisation. I've only got two bars at the moment.'

Theo insisted on paying, even though she told him she had money in her bag. She watched him joking with the barmaid as he paid the bill, and thought how much she was going to miss him when he left them. She had done something she had vowed she would never do. She had begun to rely on a man again, and that had to stop. Theo was an interlude in her life, nothing more, and soon she would have to manage without him.

She was a lot more worried about her aunt than she let on. She didn't want to upset Jake or make Theo feel he was responsible for them, but she had been trying to phone her aunt for a week now without getting a reply. At the back of her mind was the thought that Aunt Marjory might have been taken ill, or maybe even worse. When Sara had last seen her she had been in good health, but that was almost five years ago. Even four weeks ago, when Sara had asked if she could visit, her aunt had sounded fine. But now she'd stopped answering her phone, and that was a worry.

They grabbed some prepacked sandwiches at a petrol station and Theo tried Googling Marstan, the name of Aunt Marjory's village, on his iPad, but nothing came up. They were only five miles outside Norwich, but the guy behind the counter had never heard of Marstan. When Sara spelled the name out for him, he frowned for a couple of minutes, obviously thinking hard.

'You sure it's not Marston? Sounds more likely to me.'

'Is there a place called Marston near here, then?' Sara asked, thinking she could have misheard her aunt on the phone even though Marjory had spelled it out.

The young man shook his head. 'No. Not that I heard of, anyway. Lots of little places round about here with funny names. None of them on the maps. One of them got no mains water, only a well, and one don't have no broadband.' He shook his head again. 'Funny little places.'

'My goodness me,' Theo said as they drove away. 'I could manage without water, but no broadband? That would be asking too much.'

Sara laughed. 'I suppose that's what living in the sticks is all about. But my aunt has an internet connection because I've emailed her.' She was silent for a moment, her laugh turning into a frown. 'I just wish I knew why she isn't answering her phone.'

They got back in the car, and Theo suggested they find a more salubrious place to eat their sandwiches than a petrol station forecourt. 'How about finding a nice little side road somewhere so Rosie and Jake can stretch their legs and we can eat our food with the car doors open? I need to stretch my legs as well, actually. They never make cars for tall people.'

She looked down at his legs and wished she hadn't. He was wearing dark blue jeans and the fabric was stretched tight over his thighs. 'I can drive if you want me to,' she said hastily, realising she'd been staring at his legs for far too long. 'You only have to ask. You're supposed to be recuperating, not driving miles with a bullet wound in your leg. You'll make it worse.'

He turned his head to grin at her. 'No I won't. My left leg had the bullet in it and this car's automatic. My left leg has been resting the whole time, so no worries.'

Sara didn't answer him. If she did, she knew she would babble. Instead, she turned round to look at Jake. 'We'll stop somewhere nice in a little while

162

and you can get out and run around.' She could do with a run around herself. She had been sitting next to Theodore Winter for most of the morning and it was starting to addle her brain.

He found a hamlet with pretty thatched cottages scattered round a small square. He turned down a side road and discovered it was a dead end. Near the bottom of the lane, the row of farm cottages petered out and there was a gate leading into a field.

'If you stop here,' she said, 'we can eat our sandwiches in the car and Jake can take Rosie into the field for a run. I can't see any cows or sheep.'

Theo stopped the car close to the gate. 'Rosie is terrified of sheep. If one shows its face, she'll run like hell and get back in the car.'

Sara didn't tell Theo she would probably beat Rosie back to the car. She was terrified of cows. She gave Jake her usual warning about staying in sight and handed him a pack of cheese sandwiches. 'Bring the wrapper back with you; we don't leave litter in the countryside.' He shouldn't leave litter anywhere, but the qualifier made it sound more important.

She climbed out after him and stretched her arms above her head. She felt stiff and dehydrated, and she needed to know they had a bed for the night, which at the moment they didn't. She hated not having a plan. Before they left London, she thought she had everything worked out, but then they got stuck in the storm and all her carefully laid plans got blown away with the wind. Now she felt helpless, at the mercy of other people, and she hated that.

Theo opened the gate into the field and gave Rosie her favourite ball. He came back to stand beside her, much too close again, and she almost got back in the car — but then he would be even closer. She reached inside and grabbed the bag of sandwiches, handing him a pack of something. She didn't even look at the label. Perhaps if he was doing something as mundane as eating a sandwich, he wouldn't look so damned sexy.

He draped his arm across her shoulders, a friendly gesture, and she almost jumped out of her skin. For goodness sake, what was wrong with her?

'Relax,' he said. 'We're safe. Spender is miles away, wondering where you've gone.'

She couldn't tell Theo it wasn't Spender she was afraid of — it was him, and the effect he had on her. She wanted to turn round and bury herself in him. All that big, solid maleness. Something she kept reminding herself she didn't need. But then she felt his arm around her, and all her resolutions dissolved like the mist creeping over the far end of the field.

'We'll have to go soon,' she told him. 'Maybe if we bought a local map, we could find the village. If not, someone in Norwich library should be able to help us.' She missed his arm when he moved it, but she couldn't afford to get used to a male arm around her shoulders.

'Back to the main road, then,' Theo said lightly. 'Let's recall our troops and get on with the mission.'

As she walked back to the car, she looked at him worriedly. 'Don't drive back in the dark tonight, Theo. Find a hotel to stay at.'

He gave her a slow smile. 'If we can't find your aunt, we might both finish up spending the night in a hotel.'

9

Theo drove slowly through the meandering lanes back to the main road and turned the car in the direction of Norwich. He drove sedately on the inside lane while he tried to work out what he was going to do about Sara and her son. Now they were nearing their destination, he realised he didn't want to say goodbye to either of them.

When she'd stepped out of the car and closed her eyes, lifting her arms up above her head, she'd looked like the figurehead on the front of a sailing ship. The epitome of independent woman.

Sara might have decided she didn't want a man in her life, but Jake needed a father figure, and Theo suddenly realised if that role ever came up for grabs he'd have to make the biggest decision of his life. Sara wouldn't settle for a short-term relationship; she'd want the lot. Marriage, a house in the suburbs, probably with a garden, a dog for Jake — the list went on and on. If he could have kicked himself without crashing the car, he would have done. Why would he want to be lumbered with a woman and a child?

He was almost ready to go back to the job he loved. He didn't need any encumbrances. He was fine the way he was — and so was Sara.

She turned her head to look at him. 'This looks like the outskirts of the town.'

He came to with a rush, hoping he hadn't missed any red lights. 'Library,' he said, trying to get his thoughts in order. 'If we head for the centre, it should be signposted. If not we can ask.'

He pulled in outside a small news-agent's and explained what they were looking for.

'Lived here all my life,' the elderly shopkeeper told him. 'But never heard of anywhere round here by that name.

Your best bet would be the information centre. It might save you having to go into the library. Both of those places are in the Forum, and you should be able to park in the underground car park.'

The Forum was quite impressive, and Theo laughed when Jake asked if it was a palace. He stopped halfway up the steps leading to the entrance and decided the little boy had a point. The building seemed to be made mostly of glass, and once they got inside he could appreciate the sheer size of the place.

The Norwich and Norfolk Millennium Library was housed here, and so was the information centre; but although the woman they spoke to was very helpful, she had never heard of Marstan and couldn't find it on any of her maps. She even tried a search on her computer, but Theo had already done that on his laptop so he didn't expect her to do any better.

He bought a couple of maps and suggested they grab a take-away coffee and sit outside. The courtyard was sheltered and the sun was quite warm. He watched Sara wriggle out of her jacket and help Jake off with his lightweight hoody. He decided if just watching her move could turn him on, he would have to stop watching her. Concentrating on the map spread out in front of him helped him focus, but it didn't help find Aunt Marjory's village.

He folded the map and looked at Sara. She shook her head, meaning she hadn't found anything either. 'Are you sure you heard right?' he asked. 'Could you have got the name wrong?'

She shook her head again. 'I don't think so. My phone was running out of charge, but I got Aunt Marjory to spell the name for me and I repeated it to her before we got cut off. I already knew she lived somewhere in Norwich.'

'It's a pretty big place.' He thought for a moment. He had learned in the courtroom that sometimes thinking laterally was the only way to go. 'What was your uncle's first name?'

Sara looked at him as if he had gone

insane. 'What's that got to do with anything?'

'Bear with me. We aren't getting anywhere at the moment, so we need to change tactics.'

'I didn't really know my uncle because he died when I was very little, but I think his first name was Stanley.'

Theo pulled a paper napkin towards him and wrote on it, handing it to Sara. She looked at it with a frown on her face and then pushed the napkin back across the table towards him. 'You've written Marstan, and we already know that's the name of the village. I don't understand what you're getting at.'

'I've lost a lot of things in my time,' he said slowly, 'but never a whole village. It's impossible to lose a village, even a little one, so Marstan can't be the name of a village.'

'We've already talked about that. I agreed with you that it might be a street name, but the lady at the information centre couldn't find any streets with that name either.'

'If it's your aunt's address, but it's not a village and it's not a street, there's only one thing left.'

She stared at him for a moment and then dropped her head into her hands with a moan. 'It's the name of a house, isn't it? Marjory and Stanley. Marstan.' She lifted her head and looked up at him. 'I feel really stupid now. Of course it's the name of the house. When I spoke to Aunt Marjory, I remember her saying, 'This is the address, right on the edge of town,' and then she spelled out the name for me before the phone went dead. I hadn't got a street name or number, but it sounded like a village, and I thought if she'd lived there a long time someone would know her address. Goodness knows how we're going to find the place now.'

He could feel the anxiety coming off her in waves, so he reached across the table and took her hand. He had an idea he had been doing that rather a lot lately.

'As long as your aunt votes, we can

use the free search on the electoral register. We know her first and last name, and although her married name is quite common, it shouldn't be too difficult.' He gave Sara's hand a squeeze. 'Now I'm the one feeling stupid, because we could have done that in the first place before we even left the cabin.'

Sara got to her feet and told Jake to put his coat back on. 'Can we find what we want on your iPad, or do we need to go back inside to the library?'

'Let's go back to the car. They might not have a spare computer in the library, and we don't want to waste any more time.' He didn't want to remind her that if he could find Sara's aunt with only a name, so could Spender. She might think she had put the man off with her talk of King's Lynn, but Spender was a professional, and he'd probably found the Norwich address already.

Once they were back in the car, Theo reached for his tablet. Reception was good, and he found the name of the street without too much trouble. As he drove up the ramp out of the car park, he felt his stomach give a flip, and wondered if it was indigestion caused by drinking hot coffee too fast or if he was really feeling something like nerves. If it was nerves, it would be a first.

He quickly got on to the ring road and headed for the far side of the city. Jake had gone to sleep, and Sara was quiet. He wondered if he had overstepped the mark with his hand-holding, or if she had worked out the Spender problem for herself. Theo knew Sara wasn't stupid. She would have realised that Spender had probably found her aunt's address; and if he had the address, so did Cassidy.

The road was a dual carriageway, and he was trying to keep one eye on the satnav and one on the road. Sara's sudden gasp, just as the car in front braked, almost caused an accident.

'What?' he said more sharply than he intended. She had turned round in her seat and was looking behind her, and for a minute he thought there was something wrong with Jake or Rosie.

'That car . . . ' She turned and looked at him. 'The big black one that I saw go past on the other side of the road. I recognised the number plate. It belongs to Milton Cassidy.'

He risked a sideways glance at her. She looked annoyed rather than panicky. Her teeth were clenched and she had both hands balled into fists on her lap. Luckily, he could see a layby ahead and pulled in.

'Why would Cassidy be on this road, Sara? He's employed Kevin Spender to do his dirty work for him. I can't see any reason for him to follow us himself, and besides, you said he was going in the opposite direction.'

'So you don't believe me?'

'I didn't say that.' But he pretty well had, hadn't he? 'Perhaps Cassidy sold his car, or leant it to someone else.' Another sideways glance told him she had pursed her lips and was staring straight ahead. 'I'm sorry,' he said, trying to sound contrite. 'But I can't think of a reason for Cassidy to be on this road at the same time as us.'

'Neither can I, but that doesn't mean it wasn't him. The damn car has dark windows, so I couldn't see who was in it.'

'There you go, then.

'What do you mean 'there you go'? It was definitely his car. Dominic told me he paid a fortune for that number plate.'

Her voice had risen and Rosie grumbled, making Jake stir in his sleep. *Please don't wake them both up,* he prayed silently, *not while I'm trying to calm a panicking woman and find a house that probably doesn't exist.* He knew he was tired, but there was no need to take it out on Sara. If it really was Cassidy's car, the man must have a good reason to be here at this particular time. They just hadn't worked out what that reason was.

'How did you know it was Cassidy's

car?' he asked, running the risk of making her angry again.

'Because Dom used to borrow it sometimes when his father wasn't around. He liked driving the Bentley, even though he had a Porsche Cayman of his own. I think he liked having control of something his father owned. Besides, his father never drove it; he had a chauffeur.'

All right for some, Theo thought as he turned left into Aunt Marjory's road. He wasn't going to argue with Sara about what she'd seen, or thought she'd seen. He drove slowly, checking for house names. There was a mix of different styles all on one side of the road: a dozen or so detached and semi-detached houses interspersed with bungalows, all with names.

'Is it a house or a bungalow?' he asked. 'Any idea?'

'No, and I can't see the names on a lot of them,' Sara told him as she peered through the window. 'There are bushes and things in the way.'

'I'll drive to the bottom of the road and then come back up.' The road wasn't very long, and if the worst came to the worst, he would get out and check the names on foot.

'There!' she said suddenly, making Jake grumble in his sleep. 'That bungalow set back from the road behind the hedge. The name's on the gate.'

Theo backed up until they were level with the bungalow. The hedge was quite high, making it impossible to see anything on the other side.

'Stay in the car with Jake and Rosie while I check it out. It's not that late, but the place looks as if it's in darkness, at least in the front. There might be some lights on at the back, though.'

He got out of the car and walked up to the gate, pushing it open when there was no sign of activity. The place was much bigger than he had first thought — long and low, with a stout front door in the middle and two sets of windows either side. A double garage added even more length to the property. A closer look showed that although the hedge was nicely trimmed, the grass was a trifle too long, and some of the plants looked decidedly the worse for wear.

He unlatched a side gate and walked round the back. French doors opened on to a small patio, and the rest of the space was made up of curved beds and a small lawn. He peered through the windows, but it was impossible to see much. He stood back to make sure there were no lights on anywhere inside the property and then made his way back to the car. From the evidence, it was pretty obvious no one was home.

When he turned round from closing the gate, he was surprised to see a woman standing by the car talking to Sara. The passenger window had been rolled down and Rosie had her nose outside, sniffing the evening air.

The woman had been bending down to talk to Sara, but as Theo neared the car she stood up. She had slippers on her feet, white hair cut short and a smile on her face. She stood back as Sara opened the car door and swung her legs outside. Rosie didn't waste any time; she pushed through the gap as if her life depended on it and ran to squat on the grass verge.

'This is Linda, Theo,' Sara said. 'She lives next door to Aunt Marjory and saw us drive up.'

'Marjory fell over in the street a week ago and got taken to hospital,' the woman said. 'She sprained her ankle and she had a slight concussion. She was quite poorly for a few days, but she's feeling a lot better now. She asked me to keep a lookout for you and give you the key to her bungalow. You're to go in and make yourself at home. She should be out the day after tomorrow. Oh, and she said to take whatever you like from the fridge and freezer.'

'So that's why you couldn't contact her,' Theo said to Sara.

She nodded. 'If my aunt left her phone in her handbag, the hospital staff would have taken that away from her for safekeeping.'

'She asked me to let you know she was in hospital,' Linda said, 'but I couldn't find your number.' She looked at Theo apologetically. 'I'm sorry you had so much trouble finding the right place. I thought Marjory had given you directions.'

'She did,' Sara said. 'It was my mistake. Anyway, we're here now.' She took the key Linda handed to her. 'Are you sure it will be OK to let ourselves in? We'll go and see Marjory tomorrow and let her know we've arrived.'

Linda gave them another big smile. 'She'll be so pleased you arrived safely. For some reason I thought it was only you, Sara, who was coming. I didn't realise you had a husband and a little boy.'

'I work in London,' Theo said quickly before Sara had time to respond. 'But it was a long drive for Sara on her own. I'll have to get straight back, though, so I'll say goodbye now, and thank you for watching out for us. I was a bit worried when the house looked so deserted.'

The woman patted Sara on the arm. 'You all get inside before it gets really dark. You can park in front of the garage, and you have a safe drive back, Mr . . . er . . . '

'Thank you,' Theo said again. He didn't want to tell the woman his name in case anyone came around asking questions. When he didn't say anything else, she said goodbye to Sara and made her way back to her own bungalow.

'I hope I didn't sound rude, but the less we tell her the better. You need to start a new life here, Sara, and it wouldn't be a good idea to have my name linked to yours.' He got back in the car and called to Rosie, who was sniffing happily at all the new scents. 'I'll park the car in the drive and help you unpack.'

Jake was still asleep, his head lolling on his chest. He looked thoroughly uncomfortable, and Theo wondered how children managed to sleep through more or less anything and in practically any position.

Sara hadn't said a word since she said goodbye to Linda, so he'd probably said or done something to upset her, but he was too tired to work out exactly what. He made a point of parking his car just inside the driveway so no one could block his exit. He didn't really believe Sara had seen Cassidy on the Norwich road, but he wasn't taking chances. Spender could have picked up their trail somehow and followed them here.

Sara unlocked the front door while he unloaded the cases from the back of the car. Jake was moving around on his booster seat and looked as if he was about to wake up, and when Theo looked at him he opened one eye.

'Are we there?'

'Yes, we're here. Your mum has gone to open the door, so I'll carry you in and come back for the rest of the stuff.'

'I can walk by myself, thank you.' Jake pushed the button on his seat belt and got out of the car just as Sara came out through the front door.

'Good. You're awake. Come inside and sit down while I help Theo, then we'll see if we can find something to eat.'

Theo followed her inside, carrying the cases and various bags. He waited while she settled the little boy in a big armchair and handed him his tablet. Rosie jumped up beside him and settled herself at his side. When they both got back outside, Theo put his hand on her arm.

'Come on, you might as well tell me. What did I do?'

She turned towards him with her lips pressed together. She looked about as tired as he felt. 'Nothing, really.' She was silent for a long moment. 'You're not driving back tonight, are you? Not all the way back to London?'

He frowned, trying to work out what she wanted him to say. 'No, I'm too tired to drive back tonight. I'll find somewhere to stay in Norwich.'

Again the silence. Then she said, 'Why?'

'Why what?'

She gave him an angry look. 'Don't be obtuse, Theo. You know exactly what I'm talking about. I understand you want to get out of our lives as quickly as possible, I understand that perfectly, and I'm grateful for all you've done for us. But the least you could do is stay here for one night. I don't want to be on my own, not after seeing Cassidy, and I promise you can leave first thing in the morning. I didn't want to have to beg, but I will if necessary. I need to keep Jake safe, and I don't know if I can do that on my own. Not tonight, anyway.'

He wondered how he could be so stupid. He could usually read people pretty well, but she threw him every time. She had the knack of unsettling him to such an extent he couldn't even think coherently. He took a step towards her, but she backed off, holding a hand in front of her.

'No. I don't want your sympathy, just your company for one night. I've already looked, and there are three bedrooms. I want to be in the same room as Jake tonight — he needs me near him — so you can have the other guest room.'

With that, she picked up the bags from the back of the car and marched back inside the bungalow.

10

Sara hurried through to the kitchen, where she dropped the bags on the countertop. There was no way she would let him see the tears in her eyes. Did he care about them at all? He must know she was tired and scared — or perhaps he didn't. She tried so hard to be brave and confident for Jake, Theo probably thought she could cope with more or less anything on her own. It was her fault she had allowed herself to get used to having a man in her life again, and that was fatal. There wasn't a man in her life, and there probably never would be, so she had to buckle down and get on with it.

She turned as he came up behind her, ready to ward him off again, but all he did was put another bag down beside the ones she had carried in.

'Food,' he said. 'A bottle of milk, tea,

sugar and stuff. Your aunt probably has those things, but I thought we might as well use up what we brought with us.'

He was being overly polite, and she hated it. What had happened to the easy friendship from before? For a while she had thought it might be more than friendship, but he was obviously just being kind. She opened the fridge and put the milk inside. So what? He didn't have to start behaving like an idiot.

All she could hear at the moment was the sound of Jake's computer game, and that was beginning to drive her mad. She was obviously much more tired and stressed out than she had thought. She lifted an unopened bottle of wine out of a bag and looked at it with a frown. She'd been pretty sure they'd drunk all the wine before they left.

'Suppose I pour us both a glass of that?' Theo said. 'I bought it at the petrol station, so it's probably horrible, but I think we both need a glass of something.'

She could barely hear what Theo was saying over the sound of Jake's game. 'Put your earphones on, Jake,' she shouted, 'and turn the sound down before I go nuts.'

Theo held up the bottle. 'See what I mean? You need a drink.'

She managed a begrudging laugh; he already knew her too well. 'Yes, please. Vodka would be nice, but I'll settle for wine.'

Once she had the glass in her hand, she felt better. It seemed a truce had been reached. She could see lines under Theo's eyes that hadn't been there a few days ago. He looked desperately tired, and that was her doing. She couldn't ask him for anything more. If he wanted to leave tonight, she wouldn't try and stop him. She watched him pour a large glass of dark red wine for himself and felt a spark of hope. He wouldn't drive when he'd been drinking, not when he spent his life convicting others of the same offence.

'I'll see what we've got to eat. Jake gets ratty when he's hungry.'

She had turned to open the fridge door when she felt his arms go round her from behind, pulling her against him. She allowed herself to lean into him for a moment, feeling the warmth of his body against her back. She started to pull away, but he tightened his hold.

'Don't, Sara. Let me hold you. I don't want to leave you tonight, so I'll stay until your aunt gets back. But you have a new life here in Norfolk. It's a beautiful part of the country, and you deserve to be happy. Jake will love growing up here in the countryside. I work in London. London is my home, and I like the urban lifestyle.'

This time she did pull away from him. 'I'm not asking you to stay in Norfolk forever, Theo. Just for one night. To be honest, you look far too tired to go anywhere, and if you intend drinking that wine you can't drive anywhere either, so sit back and relax and help me put a meal together.'

She found oven chips in the freezer and took some eggs out of the fridge that were nearing their expiry date. Theo emptied one of the carrier bags and put an unopened pack of cheese in front of her. 'I can do cheese omelette and chips,' she told him. 'I can't find any peas, but I did find some rather sorry-looking tomatoes. They'll fry up nicely with a knob of butter. Not a very healthy combination, but to be honest, I don't care.'

The bread she'd bought two days ago was getting stale, so if she could find some dried fruit she could use up the rest of the eggs in a bread-and-butter pudding. She knew Jake liked that, and if she put it in the oven first it would be cooked by the time they finished their omelettes.

Theo patted the sofa. 'Sit down and drink your wine while the oven's heating up. We can finish the bottle with our food. We're not driving anywhere tonight.'

Aunt Marjory's living room was comfortably furnished with a large sofa and a couple of big arm chairs. She sank gratefully onto the sofa while Theo turned on the TV. He picked up the remote and sat down beside her with a sigh of contentment, his leg brushing hers. Sara knew it was only for a few hours, but she could almost imagine them as a family, watching TV while the dinner cooked.

By the time they'd finished their meal and the table had been cleared, Jake was asleep on the sofa and Theo looked as if he was about to nod off as well. She realised she must have been looking equally dozy when he offered to carry Jake to bed.

'We all need some sleep, but if you put the kettle on we can have a cup of tea before we go to bed. By the time we've drunk it, he'll be well away and you can crawl in beside him without waking him up.'

He stood with her while she eased her son out of his clothes and helped him into a pair of protective underpants and pyjama bottoms. Jake never had an accident now, even at night, but he'd been through a lot of upset recently so she travelled prepared. Better safe than sorry in someone else's bed. He opened his eyes and grumbled a few times until she put his rabbit in his arms, and then he gave a little sigh and went back to sleep.

'He'll be fine,' she said as she followed Theo outside, but right that minute she wasn't feeling particularly fine herself. The bungalow seemed unnaturally quiet, and she knew she would have been nervous if she had been on her own. Finsbury always had a background hum, even in the middle of the night, and at the cabin she had known Theo was just next door. But if her aunt had to spend any longer in hospital, Sara knew she'd have to get used to being on her own all over again, in a place as silent as the proverbial tomb and where every house seemed to back on to endless fields. Probably with cows in them.

She made tea while he made sure

everywhere was locked up, then they sat in silence while they drank it, too tired to talk.

Theo rubbed a hand over his eyes. 'I'm used to working well into the night when I have a difficult case. Usually I can manage on hardly any sleep at all. I don't know what's wrong with me.'

'Don't forget you're still getting over a serious injury. And besides, this is different.' She put her empty mug down on the coffee table. 'I've been up with Jake all night lots of times and still had to go to work the next day. It never bothered me. But like I said, this is different. I'm going to have to start over. I thought I was settled. Now all that's changed.' She stood up and walked to the window. There was only one street light and all she could see were the shadowy fields opposite. 'It was never this dark in London.'

'You'll get used to it, and when you do you'll love the peace and quiet. It's what you and Jake need right now.'

'I know that,' she said, more sharply

than she had intended. She didn't need him to remind her that she had chosen to come here, and now she had to make the best of it.

'Would you go back if you could?'

She turned to look at him. 'I couldn't afford to, not anymore. Besides, I know I'm being silly. Like you said, I'll soon get used to living in the country.'

The only reason she had been able to live near the centre of London was because she had rented a rundown apartment and made it habitable. The landlord had been happy to have her do all the decorating and repairs, but once his son took over all that changed and the rent kept going up. If she went back, she couldn't afford to live anywhere near the city, so there was no point in even thinking about it. This was her life from now on.

* * *

It would have helped if she had woken up with the sun shining, but it was pouring down with rain. Jake had spent a restless night, which meant she had as well. Now he was tucked into the small of her back, taking up most of the bed and hogging all of the duvet.

She eased away from him and crawled out of bed, grabbing her robe and slipping her feet into her slippers. There was no en-suite, so she was going to have to find the bathroom outside on the landing somewhere. She opened the bedroom door and tried to remember the layout of the bungalow, but Theo had shut all the doors when they went to bed last night and the hallway was dim in the grey early light.

She stood for a moment, undecided. The last thing she wanted to do was walk into Theo's bedroom, but she had no idea which door was which and she really needed to find the bathroom. Thinking back to the night before, she was pretty sure the bathroom was almost opposite their bedroom, so she took a chance and found she was right. She didn't want to leave Jake alone in case he woke up disorientated, so she quickly relieved herself, washed her hands and unlocked the door. She still had hold of the handle when the door was pushed open, almost hitting her in the face.

Theo stood framed in the doorway, clad only in a pair of boxers. Sara realised her mouth was hanging open and closed it hastily. His hair was all over the place and his feet were bare. He looked at her with sleepy, slightly bewildered eyes, and for one foolish moment she wanted to throw herself at him.

'The bathroom's all yours,' she said brightly, hoping her voice wasn't as unsteady as her legs. 'I'll shower later with Jake.' She waited for him to move out of her way and then practically ran back to the bedroom, shutting the door behind her.

Jake was beginning to stir, but as she walked further into the room she glanced at herself in the mirror — and wished she hadn't. She looked, she thought, like a train wreck, while Theo's hair had been attractively tousled. His chest was broad and masculine, while the gap in her robe only showed an upsetting absence of any cleavage. She knew she didn't look too bad when she made an effort, but the image in the mirror looked like something out of a horror movie. Something just risen from the dead.

Jake whimpered in his sleep and then sat bolt upright, his eyes wide open and frightened.

'It's all right, baby.' She sat on the bed and put her arms round him. 'It was only a bad dream.'

His lip quivered. 'Please can we go home, Mummy? I don't like it here.'

Neither did she much, but she knew things would get better. They had to.

By the time she took a shower and got Jake washed and dressed, Theo was already in the kitchen, coffee on the table and mugs all ready to be filled. The rain was still coming down outside, but the room was warm and filled with the smell of coffee and toast. She sat Jake at the table and found butter and marmalade in the fridge. Jake asked for jam, and a hunt in the cupboards disclosed a dozen jars filled with what looked like homemade jam. There was plum and blackberry to choose from, neither of them Jake's favourites, but Sara put a dollop of the blackberry on his plate and he didn't complain.

'I'll phone the hospital and find out when we can visit,' she said. 'Aunt Marjory might be coming home today.'

Theo buttered a slice of toast. 'I'll take you to the hospital and wait until you know what's going on.'

'There's no need. I'm sure we can get a bus. I know you want to get away.'

He gave a little huff of annoyance. 'I've told you I can stay until your aunt comes home. We can sort that out when we get to the hospital.' He glanced at Jake, who was listening to the conversation, his head turning from his mother to Theo and back again. 'Little pitchers have big ears, otherwise I'd say a lot more to you.'

I bet you would, she thought, glad Jake was in the room with them. She had a feeling Theo in a bad mood might be a little intimidating, but she wasn't in his courtroom and she didn't have to listen to him if she didn't want to.

'Where's Theo going?' Jake asked. He looked accusingly at his mother. 'You said Theo and Rosie were coming with us. They have to stay here with us. You said so.'

She kept quiet. Let Theo get himself out of this one. She wasn't going to help him. Although she did feel a little bit guilty for giving Jake the wrong idea. At the time she hadn't thought any further than the journey.

'I have to go to work, Jake,' Theo said. 'And I work in London.'

'But you're coming back after you finish work.'

It hadn't been a question, Sara realised. It had been a statement of fact. She felt sorry for Theo. She had been on the receiving end of more than one of Jake's interrogations, and he seemed to be proving a match for the lawyer.

'Theo may have to stay in London for a bit,' she said. It wasn't fair to let Theo suffer at the hands of her four-year-old son. 'He's got a lot of work to catch up on.'

Jake thought for a minute, his mouth pursed. 'Rosie can stay with us, then. She doesn't have to go to work, and she likes it here.'

'But your aunt may not like dogs,' Theo answered carefully.

'Of course she does,' Jake said. 'Everyone likes dogs.' As far as he was concerned, that was an indisputable fact and ended the argument.

Theo was about to answer, but Sara gave an almost imperceptible shake of her head. If he kept on he was going to lose. Sometimes it paid to give in gracefully.

'I'll phone the hospital and find out if we can visit.'

She picked up her phone and held up

her hand for silence while she dialled the number. She watched Jake go back to his toast and milk quite happily. He seemed to believe everything had been decided.

Sara spoke for a few minutes and then put her phone down. 'We can visit from eleven until twelve. By that time, the consultant will have seen my aunt and we'll know when she's coming home. She has her lunch at twelve, so we have to be sure to leave on time.' Sara grinned. 'The woman I spoke to is in charge of the ward, and she sounded like my old headmistress. If we don't do exactly as we're told, I think we might have to do detention.'

By the time everyone was dressed and the kitchen tidied up, it was time to start out for the hospital. Theo had taken Rosie outside and then put her rug on the armchair. She looked settled for the morning. According to Theo's Google search, there was only one hospital in the town, so it should be easy to find. Surprisingly for an old market town, the hospital was a modern structure of metal and glass with nicely landscaped grounds and little walkways wide enough for a wheelchair. Aunty Marjory, they discovered, was in the private wing at the back of the building.

The dragon Sara had spoken to on the phone wasn't around, and she was shown to her aunt's room by a nice, friendly nurse. Theo had agreed to stay outside with Jake until Sara had a chance to explain why she wasn't on her own.

'Good morning, Mrs Driver,' the nurse said. 'Your niece is here. You have about half an hour,' she told Sara, 'and then Mrs Driver will be having her lunch. If you need me, I'll be right outside.'

Sara had forgotten how imposing her aunt could be. Marjory Driver was not in her bed; instead she was sitting by the window with a book on her lap. She was a large lady with thick white hair and plump arms, which she immediately wrapped round Sara. Her leg was propped on a stool, her foot in plaster.

'It's been too long, Sara. You should have come to see me before this, but I suppose London is more exciting than this out-of-the way spot.' She didn't give Sara time to answer. 'Anyway, you're here now, and you can stay with me as long as you like.'

'I'm not on my own,' Sara said. There was no easy way to break the news. 'I have a son. He's almost five years old and he's waiting outside.'

Marjory's sharp blue eyes opened wide, and then she smiled. 'Oh, Sara, I'm so pleased for you. No wonder you didn't visit sooner. Fetch him in right this minute. I can't wait to meet him. Why on earth didn't you tell me?'

Sara opened the door and called to Theo to bring Jake in. 'It's complicated,' she said.

Jake came in holding Theo's hand, and stopped nervously when he saw Marjory. She didn't make the mistake of holding out her arms; instead she tipped her head on one side and studied him. He squirmed for a minute and then said, 'Are you my Aunty Marjory?'

The woman nodded. 'Yes, I am. I'm your Great-aunt Marjory. I hurt my foot, but a nice doctor mended it for me. Do you want to write your name on my plaster?'

She picked up a pen from the bedside table and held it out to him. He looked at his mother for permission and then took the pen. He had recently learned how to write his name and he was very proud of his new ability. He walked over to Marjory and looked at the white plaster, and then he wrote his name slowly and carefully, mouthing each letter to himself as he went. When he'd finished he stood back and waited expectantly.

Aunt Marjory leaned forward and looked at her leg. 'Jake Finch. Is that your name?' When he nodded, she gave him a satisfied smile. 'Good. If I can read your name, it shows how well you can write.'

Beaming with pride, Jake sat on the bed beside her and she turned her attention to Theo.

'I assume you're Jake's father, young man.'

11

Sara and Theo both started to speak at once and Aunt Marjory held up her hand. 'If you both talk at the same time, I can't understand either of you.'

'Theo is a friend,' Sara said. 'He kindly offered to bring us both here, but he has to return to London in a couple of days.'

'So I take it the answer to my question is no?' When Sara nodded, she said, 'Well, he jolly well should be. He's ridiculously handsome, and if he's not already married you'd be a fool to let him out of your sight.' She scooped Jake off the bed before he had time to get away and sat him on her lap. Sara was amazed when he didn't complain. 'But you already said it's complicated, so that story will have to keep for later. My lunch will be here soon. The consultant says I can leave tomorrow morning after his visit. He wants to put a new, more comfortable strapping on my foot.' She turned her penetrating blue eyes on Theo. 'So I shall need a lift home tomorrow, young man, if that's not too much trouble.'

'Not at all, Mrs Driver. I'd be delighted. Besides, I slept in your house last night, so that's the least I can do.'

Sara watched him being charming and wondered if it was an act or if he had been born that way. A bit of both probably, she decided. His striking looks were hereditary, but the charm had most likely been learned in the courtroom.

'Don't even think of having lunch in the hospital canteen. It's like something out of World War Two. Take a drive round the villages; there are some lovely places to eat just outside the town.' Marjory looked at the window. 'It's stopped raining and the sun's out, so it should be nice.'

Once they were back in the car, Theo turned on the engine and looked at the display on the dashboard. 'According to my satnav, there's a riverside pub somewhere near here. Shall we eat out by the river? My treat. We may not see one another again for a while.'

'Until you get home from work, Theo,' Jake said. 'Can I have a burger and chips, Mummy?'

Glad of the change of subject, Sara decided she might as well make the most of the situation. She didn't want him to stay. She didn't need him involved in their lives. Like he said, this was a new start. While she looked for somewhere permanent to stay, she had to get a job and enrol Jake in a good school. There wouldn't be time to worry about anything else. Although she did wonder what Theo meant by 'for a while'.

The pub was lovely, exactly what a riverside country pub should be like: An old coach house with low beams and trestle tables right beside the river. Jake didn't get his burger, but he was more than content with a child-size plate of fish and chips. She remembered going to places like this with her parents when she was a child. When she remembered her childhood, it always seemed to be sunny, the school holidays filled with exciting days out and picnics by the river.

Theo was sitting quietly, watching the ducks on the water. He was wearing lightweight black combat trousers and a pale grey t-shirt that almost matched his eyes. She'd miss those eyes. Rosie was sprawled out under the table while Jake dropped blades of grass in the water and watched them sail away. She suddenly felt a gut-wrenching ache for a proper family life: Days like this, having lunch by the river, the dog asleep at their feet, watching their son play happily on the grassy bank.

'You look sad,' Theo said, and she realised he'd been watching her.

'I'm not sad. Just the opposite, in fact. I was thinking what a lovely day it's been. I'll be sure to bring Jake here again.'

'By yourself?'

'I'm used to being by myself, but you never know what's round the corner.'

'Jake's getting older. It would be good for him to have a man around.'

'But it's not a necessity, is it? I'm sure I can turn him into a well-rounded, kind, loving human being without any help from a man.'

'I'm sure you can.' He narrowed his eyes. 'But he's going to need a certain amount of toughness if he's going to succeed out there in the big world. He's a boy, Sara, and in case you haven't noticed, boys are different from girls.'

'If you're trying to tell me Jake needs a father, it's a bit late for that. His father is dead. And at the moment there don't seem to be any other men on the scene.' *Not stayers, anyway,* she thought bitterly. All the men she knew walked away when the going got tough.

They drove back in silence. Why did men think they were a necessity? She would not go to pieces when Theo left. She had spent five years turning herself into the woman she was now. Jake seemed to be doing fine, although the test would come when he started proper school. If she could get through this week, she could start putting her life back together again.

When Theo turned into her aunt's little cul-de-sac, Sara noticed a car parked outside Aunt Marjory's bungalow. It started up as soon as Theo turned the corner and headed back out onto the main road. She felt the adrenaline kick in. Paranoia again? Or was it her heightened sense of self-preservation? When she looked at Theo, he was frowning.

'Not the Vauxhall,' she said. 'So not Spender. Not unless he's changed his car.'

Theo pulled up and turned to look at her. 'Just someone who decided to park by the side of the road. It happens. It doesn't have to mean anything sinister.'

'So why were you frowning?'

He got out of the car and came round to open her door. 'Because you're beginning to make me as jumpy as you. It was nothing, Sara. And anyway, now they've gone.'

'Did you get the registration number?'

'No,' he said evenly. 'Did you?'

She ignored him and helped Jake out, making sure he had his rabbit and his android tablet. She couldn't afford another one of those.

Theo walked in ahead of her and she heard him filling the kettle in the kitchen. She envied him his ability to make himself at home wherever he was. She could imagine him in the court-room looking completely relaxed, while his razor-sharp brain worked overtime on some complicated case. Now and again an edge of ruthlessness showed through his easy-going exterior, and she decided she wouldn't want to be on the losing side in any confrontation with The Ice Man.

Jake had already eaten enough to keep him going, so Sara gave him a biscuit and a mug of warm milk to help him sleep. Theo poured the tea and they finished off the biscuits between them. Then he suddenly got to his feet and said he was taking Rosie up the road for a walk. Sara watched him put on his jacket and put his cap on his head, pulling the peak down over his eyes.

Sara gave him a curious look. 'The sun has gone in, Theo. It's already getting dark outside.'

'I know.'

'Can I come?' Jake asked.

She shook her head. 'No, it's getting late and you've got to have a bath. There's a proper bath here, so we can put some bubbles in it if you like.'

'I won't be long,' Theo said, and disappeared through the kitchen door.

Sara wondered why he had gone out the back, but it was none of her business, so she got Jake undressed and let him play in the bath for a little while. She heard Theo come back but he didn't come to find them. She got Jake bathed and into bed and then called to Theo to come and say goodnight. Rosie came bounding in as well, and Theo only just managed to stop her jumping on the bed.

'Dirty feet,' he told Jake. 'You wouldn't want her in bed with you.'

'Yes, I would.'

'Don't argue,' Sara told her son, dropping a kiss on the tip of his nose. 'Go to sleep now. Tomorrow we're going to pick up Aunty Marjory.'

She followed Theo back into the hallway. Something was wrong, but she couldn't imagine what. He had only been out about twenty minutes.

Once they were in the living room, she shut the door. Whatever was going on, Jake didn't need to know about it. She turned to Theo and saw the frown was back on his face.

'What?'

He sat down on the sofa and patted the seat beside him. She was never quite sure whether to be insulted or pleased by that gesture, but she sat as requested.

'You know the car that was parked outside when we got back?'

She nodded, a slightly sick feeling settling in her stomach. 'The one that drove away as soon as it saw us.'

'Well, it's back. That's why I went out — to make sure it had gone.'

'And it hasn't?'

'No. It's parked at the end of the road with its lights off and two men sitting inside it. I don't suppose it means anything. Just two men sitting in a car.'

'But you obviously think it does mean something, or you wouldn't have mentioned it. Did someone take over from Spender, do you think? Are they here to find out where I live? Is someone always going to be following me? What's the matter with Milton Cassidy? Why won't he leave me alone?'

Theo held up his hand to silence her as if they were in a courtroom, and she wanted to slap him. She had a right to voice her fears. She was feeling completely freaked out again, and that was his fault. If the two men in the car were nothing, why had he bothered to tell her about them?

'I should have searched my car before we left,' he said. 'The only way we could have been followed is if there is a tracker on my car as well. I was being particularly naive. You can get hold of those little tracking devices quite easily and they're relatively cheap. If he was going to put one on your car, it would make sense to put one on mine as well. Spender saw us together at the lake. He probably thought we were an item.'

'But we came in different cars, at different times, and rented separate cabins.'

'I suppose it would make some sort of sense if I was having an affair with you and didn't want my wife to find out; but I agree, it's stretching plausibility a bit.'

'So you're telling me I've got nothing to worry about?'

'Not a thing. Besides, you've got me

sleeping in the bedroom next door to you.'

She managed a smile. 'Now you've got me even more worried.'

But she did sleep better knowing he was in the room next door. She got out of bed once to take Jake to the toilet, but he went straight back to sleep again, and the next time she opened her eyes sunshine was streaming in the window.

She pushed it wide open and listened to the early-morning chorus of birds. One of them sounded very much like the blackbird they had listened to from the window of the flat, but she doubted that particular bird had followed them from London. She decided to slip into the bathroom before Jake woke up, but this time she listened at the door to make sure Theo wasn't already inside. Ten minutes later, after a quick shower, she opened the door and came face to face with him.

He was almost naked again; the hand towel wrapped round his waist hardly covered the bare essentials. Damn the man, he had no right to look that fabulous so early in the morning.

She grabbed the top of her robe with one hand and pulled the sash round her waist tighter with the other, feeling like a complete nincompoop. No makeup and wet hair always made her feel like that.

His eyes travelled slowly from the top of her head to the tips of her toes and then back up again. When his eyes locked on hers, she could feel her face starting to heat up.

'Have you seen enough?' she asked caustically, hoping he'd hurry up and get out of her way.

'No, but it will do for now. We'll have to stop meeting like this. I can never think of anything remotely intelligent to say when you're standing in front of me all damp and delicious.'

'You don't have to say anything. Just move so I can get past and you can have the whole bathroom to yourself. Besides, you shouldn't be standing out here wearing nothing but a towel. What if Aunt Marjory should come out of her room and see you?'

He grinned at her. 'It would probably make her day. My bedroom door is right next to the bathroom, so I wouldn't be standing out here if you hadn't stopped me.'

With an irritated little huff, she pushed past him and hurried back to her room. There had been some skin contact when she brushed against him, and she was feeling decidedly warm. She closed the bedroom door and leaned against it, waiting for her heart to stop racing. She had seen half-naked men before. There had been lots of them at the lido when she had taken Jake for a day out. The local swimming team wore little stretchy Lycra numbers that left very little to the imagination. So why did the sight of Theo in a towel send her straight into a spin?

'Are you all right, Mummy?'

Jake was sitting up in bed looking at her curiously. 'I'm fine, poppet,' she told him, feeling anything but. 'I've had a quick shower, but you can have a bath if you like.'

He shook his head. 'I had a bath before I went to bed, and I didn't get dirty in bed, so I don't need another one.'

Giving in to her son's impeccable logic, she helped him have a wash-down and laid out his clothes for the day. She wanted to make sure she got to the kitchen first this time so she could make the coffee and show her independence. Ridiculous, she knew, but she had allowed Theo to take over some of the jobs that were normally hers, and that had to stop as well. The first thing she would do when he went back to London was start looking for somewhere to rent locally. She didn't want to depend on Aunt Marjory for any longer than necessary.

Jake liked dressing himself, and she had started teaching him how to do up buttons and tie shoe laces. All his shoes and trainers had Velcro fasteners at the moment, but there would no doubt come a time when he would need to be able to tie a bow. He loved being able to manage by himself, but it took him a long time, and she could smell the coffee as soon as she opened the bedroom door. Theo had beaten her to it again.

'It's gone,' he said as soon as she walked into the kitchen.

She shook her head, confused. 'What's gone?'

'The car,' he said a little impatiently. 'The one we were talking about last night. It's not anywhere around as far as I can see. I took Rosie for a run before I had my shower so I could check.'

So he had been worrying about the two men in the car. She had a feeling she was missing something. She lifted Jake onto a seat at the table and put a slice of bread in the toaster. Theo handed her a mug of steaming coffee and she added milk from the jug he had filled.

'What aren't you telling me, Theo?'

He blinked at her. 'I don't know what you mean.'

'You can drop the innocent look. You're more worried about that car than you should be. Like you said, it was just two men sitting in a car. Not even in this road, but round the corner. So I'll say it again. What aren't you telling me?'

The toast popped up and Theo put it on Jake's plate. He buttered it without thinking. Sara added a spoonful of jam and watched Jake spread it over his toast.

'I think I recognised the driver of the car,' he said. 'Well, not recognised, exactly, but I'm sure I've seen him somewhere before. The other man was bending down when I went past so I couldn't get a good look at him.'

She shook her head. 'That's not possible. If they've been following me, why would you know one of them? Even if they haven't been following me, even if they're nothing to do with

223

Spender or Milton Cassidy, they were sitting outside Aunt Marjory's bungalow. That's pushing coincidence a bit too far, isn't it?'

'Yes, of course it is. I must have been mistaken,' he said reassuringly. 'I was once told there are only five faces. We all have a face that is a variation of one of those five, so everyone looks a little bit like someone else.'

He was trying to put her mind at rest, she thought. Probably wishing he hadn't said anything. But she could tell he was still worried. The whole thing was crazy. None of it made any sense anymore.

'Does Jake's grandfather have enough evidence to take me to court? Does he have enough to prove I'm not fit to look after his grandson?'

Theo shook his head. 'Not in a million years, Sara. Besides, if he even considers taking you to court, he'd have me to contend with.'

'He can get the best lawyers in the country.'

Theo shook his head again. 'No he can't. I told you before, *I'm* the best lawyer in this country.'

She couldn't help smiling. The arrogance of the man was amazing. 'Are you quite sure about that?'

He grinned at her. 'Yes, I am, but we won't ever have to put it to the test. Not as far as you and Jake are concerned, anyway.'

Jake finished his jammy toast and ran his fingers through his hair before wiping them on his shorts. *That should get the jam off*, she thought resignedly. 'If you put messy fingers in your hair one more time, I'll have your head shaved. Then you won't have any hair left to wipe them on.'

Jake looked up at her, wide-eyed. 'Will you really? If I have my head shaved, I'll look like that man on TV. It'll be really cool.'

Theo laughed out loud. 'I use that ploy sometimes in court. If you agree with your opponent, it throws him right off course.'

Sara pulled a face at him, and then she turned back to her son. 'I might decide to chop your fingers off instead, so don't push me too far, young man.' She lifted him down from his chair. 'Off to the bathroom with you. But I mean it, this is the last time I let you get away with being a horrible messy child.'

'But I have to do it again to get my head shaved.'

He squealed and ran for the door as she chased him to the bathroom. As she washed his hair over the bath, she wondered if little girls put jam in their hair as well, or if it was just a boy thing.

Sara had been told her aunt wouldn't be ready to come home until lunch time, but she phoned the hospital to see if she could get a definite time to collect Marjory. She didn't want to keep the poor woman hanging about waiting once she was told she could come home. About twelve midday, definitely not before, was the best the hospital could do, so she vacuumed and tidied up the bungalow while Theo took Rosie and Jake out for a walk. She had a feeling he wanted to check that the strange car had really gone, and she wondered again if there was something more he wasn't telling her.

Milton Cassidy had sent Spender to take some photos that would prove she was incapable of looking after his grandson. That she could understand, but he could have hired someone to take those photos in London; she had been much more vulnerable there. Her landlord had put their belongings out on the doorstep and she hadn't seen anyone taking photos then. A picture of her loading up the car with Jake crying because he didn't want to leave his friends — that would have made a good case against her. Maybe there had been someone taking photos and she hadn't seen them, but in that case why follow her all the way to Norfolk? And what was Milton Cassidy doing in the area? She was quite sure she had seen him on the road near Norwich, even if Theo didn't believe her.

Another coincidence? She didn't think so. There had to be more to it.

When Theo came back, she knew he was still worried about something. 'What is it?' she said. 'Is the car back outside? Tell me.'

'No, I didn't see the car anywhere. You've got nothing to worry about.'

She threw up her hands in exasperation. 'So what is it, then? If you don't tell me, Theo, I'll worry even more.'

'The man I saw in the car looked like a thug, Sara, and from what you've told me about Milton Cassidy he wouldn't employ thugs.'

'Maybe he didn't know he was employing thugs. Maybe Spender employed those two men, or maybe it was Spender in the car with a friend. You said you only got a look at one of them.'

He shrugged. 'It's possible, but it's much more likely that they have nothing to do with your grandfather and you're worrying about nothing.'

'You're sure they've gone?'

'As sure as I can be.'

That wasn't the answer she wanted, but she realised he couldn't truthfully give her more, and she had asked for the truth.

He was wearing light blue jeans and a polo shirt, and sandals on his bare feet, and for a moment she wondered what he would look like in his business gear. He had been wearing a dark suit when she had seen him on TV, his hair slicked back from his face, and he had looked completely different. She frowned, remembering he had said he recognised one of the men and, from what she had read about The Ice Man, he mixed with thugs every day of the week. One of those thugs had shot him.

12

Jake and Sara were both ready to leave for the hospital, and Rosie was prancing excitedly round by the front door. As they weren't going to be long at the hospital, Theo had decided the little dog could come with them. All he had to do was put on his shoes, but he hesitated. An alarm bell in his head told him something wasn't quite right, and he had become used to trusting that mental alarm bell. But the car had gone. He had made sure of that on his walk, going further than he needed to so he could check round every corner and in every driveway. So what was he worrying about?

'You ready?' Sara said, and he nodded, pulling his car keys out of his pocket.

'It's funny,' he said, 'how you can look at someone and think you've seen them before — be pretty damn sure, in fact — but I know from my court cases how easy it is to be mistaken.'

'I thought I saw Milton Cassidy following us in Norwich; but as you kindly pointed out, I was mistaken as well.'

'The Bentley was going in the other direction, Sara. Not exactly following us.' He saw the expression on her face and held up a hand in surrender. 'So we were both wrong. Let's leave it at that, shall we?'

He couldn't understand why women had to beat a subject to death. He had admitted he might possibly be wrong. That should have been enough. He wasn't going to tell her that he was still sure he had seen the man somewhere before. It was definitely someone he knew by sight. If he looked at it logically, and the man in the car was just someone he had come across in the past, then coincidence did play a part. He once met an old girlfriend while he was walking down a street in India. You meet people you know all the time — and in all sorts of places.

Sara was waiting by the front door, a resigned look on her face. She irritated him beyond endurance sometimes. What he saw in her that was so fascinating, he had no idea. She was quite pretty, he supposed, with all that dark wavy hair and those golden-brown eyes, but he had met women far prettier. Maybe it was the stubborn streak in her nature, the fact that she was still fighting back in spite of everything that had been thrown at her. Or maybe it was just a sexual thing, because he fancied her like crazy, even when she was annoying the hell out of him. Probably all of the above, he thought as he took Jake's hand and followed her out of the door.

Aunt Marjory was waiting for them in the hospital lobby. Her leg was strapped from ankle to knee, and some sort of walking machine was standing beside her. She didn't look happy.

'I'm sorry if we're late,' Sara said. 'I

was told not to come before twelve o'clock. Have you been waiting long?'

'No, only a few minutes. It's not that, dear. I thought I was going to be able to walk, even if I was still strapped up; but now I've been told I mustn't put too much weight on my ankle.' She waved a hand at the walker. 'I can't manage on crutches — keep falling over the damn things — so they've given me this silly contraption.'

'You could have asked for a wheel-chair, Aunty,' Theo suggested. 'I won a wheelchair race at university. We could have had some fun.'

Aunt Marjory looked at Sara. 'You don't seem to have much control over this one.'

'None at all,' Sara said. 'Do you need some help getting up?'

'No, child, I do not. And if you think I'm going to let you run around after me once we get home, you'll have to pack your bags and leave.'

Theo stifled a chuckle. Aunt Marjory definitely had a way with her.

A slightly harassed nurse appeared at her side. 'Let me help you up, Mrs Driver. You mustn't put weight on your foot.'

Marjory grabbed hold of the walker and pulled herself to her feet. 'I'm quite capable of getting out of a chair on my own, and this thing is called a walker, so presumably it's supposedto help me to walk. But if I can't put any weight on my foot, I shall have to hop.' She began hopping towards the exit sign, and the nurse rolled her eyes heavenwards.

'You can walk holding on to the walker, but put as little weight on your ankle as possible. Otherwise you'll be straight back in here so we can put a plaster cast on your foot again, and you won't be able to walk properly for goodness knows how long.'

Marjory looked at Theo. 'You're a lawyer, and you heard that, didn't you? Everyone knows about the bullying that goes on in hospitals.' She put her strapped foot on the floor and winced. 'But I assure you,' she said to the nurse,

'I shall be very careful not to put too much weight on my bad foot. I certainly don't want to end up in here again.'

Theo held the door for Sara's aunt, very glad he wasn't the one having to look after her. He had a feeling she would be quite a handful. He would leave the following day and get back to his life in London. Sara was walking close to her aunt in case there were any accidents, and Theo felt Jake's hand slide into his. At the moment he had no idea how he was going to explain his departure to the little boy.

There were a number of corridors to negotiate, and by the time they reached the car park Marjory had slowed almost to a standstill. By the look on her face, she was wishing she had taken Theo up on his suggestion and asked for a wheelchair.

The small hospital car park was quite full, but Theo had managed to find a parking space at the far end. Sara settled her aunt on a convenient seat and suggested Theo go to get the car. Jake had Rosie on her lead and was walking on the grass verge off to one side near a row of parked cars. He had already disappeared from sight a couple of times between cars and she had to call to him.

'If you won't stay in sight, Jake, you'll have to come over here and sit on the seat.'

Theo headed towards where he had parked the car. 'Do what your mother says, Jake. A car park is always dangerous. You might get run over.'

Jake stood still, an obstinate look on his face, and Theo thought how much like his mother he looked right at that moment.

'I just want to see the puppies,' he said, and disappeared again.

Theo glanced at Sara and saw the worried look on her face. She didn't want to leave her aunt, but every basic instinct in her body was telling her to run after her child.

'Jake, come back here this minute,' she called.

'Stay there. I'll get him.' Theo started for the space between two parked cars where he had last seen Jake, but at that moment Rosie started barking furiously and a car engine came to life with a roar. Theo broke into a run, but a gut instinct told him he was going to be too late. Jake had said something about puppies, and that was one of the oldest ploys in the world to entice a child into a car.

As he rounded the back of a large off-roader, he saw the car making all the noise. It was a small black Toyota, the same car that had been parked outside the bungalow. The engine was revving furiously, but the back passenger door was still open, and he caught a glimpse of Jake inside. For a moment he thought he might get there in time. He was actually reaching out for the open door when someone slammed it from inside and the car raced away. Rosie was about to run after it, but

Theo stepped on her trailing lead and stopped her.

He watched the car for a couple of seconds before he realised it had been going the wrong way. There was only one exit from the car park, so the car was going to have to turn around and come back past him.

He looked back at Sara and knew immediately what was going to happen. He could see the scenario playing out in his head. But as he reached the spot where Sara was standing, the car came hurtling back towards them; and just as he had known she would, Sara ran into the middle of the road and held out her arms.

Somewhere in his distant past, Theo had spent hours training to get a place on the university rugby team. He had never been quite good enough, but now he threw himself at Sara, caught her round her waist, and launched himself at the grassy verge where Jake had been playing. He knew he was going to come down hard, but he managed to turn his body so Sara was on top of him. At any other time he might have enjoyed the experience, but Sara pushed herself up and got away from him, planting her heeled shoe in the middle of his chest, making him grunt with pain. She was revving on adrenalin and ran over to her aunt without looking back.

There had been a noise, he realised. A loud noise. A crunch of metal and a squeal of brakes, and he thought for a moment the black car had hit something. As he got to his feet, he realised it had done exactly that. When he had grabbed Sara, Aunt Marjory had pushed her walker in front of the escaping vehicle, and now bits of metal were scattered all over the road. Some of the debris belonged to the walker, but not all of it. Most of the exhaust system and the plastic parts of the car's rear end had fallen off. He could still hear it labouring loudly up the road away from the hospital. For a moment he considered going after it on foot, but he had no hope of catching it unless it broke down completely, and Sara was going to be traumatised. Even if she didn't know it, she needed him.

He took his phone out of his pocket, praying it wasn't damaged, and dialled 999.

Two policemen in a first response vehicle were there in ten minutes. What seemed like half the staff from the hospital had gathered outside in case anyone was injured, but when the police questioned them no one had actually seen anything. They had just heard all the noise.

Sara was surprisingly calm. 'If Jake's grandfather has taken him, he won't be harmed,' she said quietly to Theo. The younger of the two policemen asked her to give her account of exactly what had happened, and she did so slowly and concisely.

'I believe my son's grandfather arranged for his abduction. Milton Cassidy has been having me followed for the past month. His son, Jake's father, died recently and Milton wants custody of his grandson.'

The policeman, whose name was Webster, looked uncomfortable. 'So you think a family member took the boy?'

Sara frowned. 'He's not a family member. He wanted nothing to do with Jake when he was born.'

The young man looked at his colleague for help, but Theo stepped in. He didn't want this to get any more complicated than it already was. 'Even if a family member was involved, these two men had no right to abduct a four-year-old child without his mother's consent.'

'Do you have any proof the boy was taken by his grandfather?' the older of the two policeman asked.

'We've got proof,' Sara said. 'Cassidy sent someone to follow me and he put a tracker on my car. He used a security firm called Spender Investigations, and although I only got a glimpse of them, one of the two men in the car looked like Mr Spender.'

She looked beseechingly at the older of the two policemen. 'It doesn't matter who took him; they can't have got far in that car. It was making a dreadful noise. Someone needs to go after them.'

'Someone will,' the older of the two policemen said soothingly. 'I phoned in the details on our way here. Your husband gave us a good account of the state of the car, and someone is already out looking for it. We'll find your son, Mrs Finch. Like you said, he can't be far away.'

Sara didn't contradict the policeman about having a husband, so Theo didn't either. It wasn't the first time he had been taken for her husband, and he was beginning to quite enjoy the experience. He told them about the two men he had seen parked outside the bungalow, and gave a rough description of the driver, the man he had seen when he walked past the car in Marjory's road.

'They won't get far.' The young policemen looked at the bits littering the car park and kicked a piece of exhaust. 'It's a wonder they managed to drive away.'

Theo was inclined to agree with him. A message had already been sent out giving a description of the car. But what he was worrying about was what would happen to Jake when the car packed up and the two men had to ditch it. It was all very well for Sara to say Milton Cassidy wouldn't hurt his grandchild, but Milton Cassidy wasn't the one who had taken Jake. The car was likely to grind to a halt any minute, and they would have to leave it by the roadside. He had only seen the men for a couple of seconds, but Jake would have a much better idea of what both men looked like, and that could put the little boy's life in danger.

He wondered if he should have told the police his suspicions; but if he was wrong, those suspicions would muddy the waters and could hold up the search operation. At the moment it seemed more prudent to keep things simple. Besides, he had no proof. Not yet.

Sara wanted to drive around looking for her son, and Theo could understand why; he wanted to look for Jake as well. The local police would do all they could, but they had limited facilities, and Norwich Police Force wouldn't get involved unless Jake was still missing when it got dark.

'We'll drop you and Rosie back at the bungalow and then go look for Jake,' he told Marjory, but she was having none of it.

'Don't waste time on me,' she said. 'They've got a nice coffee shop here. I'll be fine until you get back. You can take the little dog with you. Use her as a sniffer dog.'

Five minutes later, they were following the trail of oil Jake's kidnappers had left on the road.

'Those policemen are like everyone else,' Sara said bitterly. 'They won't believe anything I say about Milton Cassidy.'

'Why do you think that?'

'Because I have no proof, Theo. As soon as I start accusing Milton Cassidy of kidnapping, they think I've gone mad. I can't really believe it myself. Why would he do something like that? He must know he can't get away with it.'

He turned his head to glance at her and saw her eyes were wide with fear.

'He can't get away with it, can he?'

'No, not if it really is Cassidy who took Jake. Like you said, it seems a silly thing to do. He may be Jake's grandfather, but he can't take him away without your permission.'

'It must be Milton. Who else would want to take Jake? Do you think it was some pervert waiting to trap a little boy? That would be a bit of a coincidence, after everything else that's happened.'

He had been trying to put her mind at rest, but he realised he had probably done just the opposite. She had been sure that Cassidy wouldn't hurt Jake, but now he had put the idea in her head that someone else could be responsible for her son's abduction — which, in retrospect, was a pointless thing to do. He still hadn't managed to get a good look at both the men in the car, so he had probably worried her for no reason. When the car was hurtling towards him, his priority had been to get Sara out of the way, not look at the driver's face; and when he had walked towards the open door, he had been trying to see if Jake was in the car, not mentally photographing the other occupants. One thing he was sure of — there had never been any puppies.

'How far could they have got?' Sara was staring out of the window as if her life depended on it. 'The car barely made it out of the car park; surely it can't have got far.'

'They won't take it as far as the main road, it would be too risky. They'd likely get stopped by a police car, or reported by a responsible citizen. They'll ditch it before then.'

'They could get a lift if they were on their own.' She turned to look at Theo. 'But not if they have Jake with them. He wouldn't keep quiet, you know that. What will they do with him?'

'Drop him off somewhere, maybe outside a house; and if they do that the people who find him will phone the police. He'll be OK, Sara.'

Theo wished he felt as confident as he sounded. He had no idea how the minds of the two men would work. When he told Sara they would drop Jake off, he had a vision of the little boy being pushed from the moving car, and if that happened the child could very well be seriously injured. Theo's eyes scanned the banks beside the road as anxiously as hers. He didn't know what to say to make her feel better.

He kept heading towards the main road. He felt sure the men would dump the car and try and get a lift, and Sara was right, they couldn't risk trying to get a lift if they had Jake with them. He glanced at her and saw she was clutching the parcel shelf in front of her, her knuckles white.

'I always make him hold my hand if we're walking beside a road. He doesn't have much road sense yet.'

The secondary road they were on had little traffic, but what it did have was moving quite fast. Theo drove slowly, hoping to see something that would tell him he was on the right track, another piece of debris from the car or the car itself. Every now and again a car hooted behind him, or overtook impatiently. Talking to the police had taken longer than he expected, and the light was fading fast. The thought of Jake out on his own in the dark filled Theo with horror. The little boy was only four years old, and being on his own beside a fast road at night would be just as dangerous as being with the two men, if not more so.

'Look! Sara said suddenly. She pointed to a large piece of metal by the side of the road. 'What's that?'

Theo put his hazard lights on and slowed some more. 'It looks like the last piece of the exhaust. The car will be full of fumes from the engine, so they'll have to leave it and get out before they get poisoned.' Sara didn't say anything, and he cursed his runaway tongue. She didn't need to know any of that.

They found the car just round the next bend. The men had managed to get it halfway up onto the verge so it wasn't too much of a hazard to other drivers, and Theo was sure someone would have phoned it in by now. In this age of phones and tablets and with Bluetooth built into the cars, nothing went unreported for long.

Sara was out almost before he had stopped. She ran to the other car and looked inside. She turned to look at him and shook her head. This stretch of road was devoid of houses. A narrow grass verge divided the road from fields full of rape, just beginning to turn yellow, bright in the evening sun. Sara stood looking across the field. The crops weren't thick enough to hide anything, and there was no reason to suppose Jake would start walking through the plants. If he was walking anywhere, he would follow the road.

'He's not here and we didn't pass him anywhere, so what have they done with him?'

'They may have taken him with them, but it's more likely they left him somewhere and tried to wave down a passing motorist. If they stood by the car, someone would give them a lift, but I can't see Jake keeping quiet if they kept him with them.'

'So they probably ditched him somewhere.'

She was standing beside the broken-down car, her face in shadow. He needed to see how she was coping with this development, so he walked over to her and tipped up her chin. She wasn't crying, but her eyes were glistening with unshed tears and he took her in his arms. He was expecting resistance, but she relaxed against him, resting her head on his shoulder.

'I don't know what to do, Theo.'

He held her against him, stroking her hair. 'We will find him, Sara.' He desperately wanted to believe what he was saying. He loved the little boy, and he was fast falling in love with Jake's mother. There was no way he could walk away. Particularly as he had realised that all this — Kevin Spender, the men in the car, and Jake's abduction — might be his fault.

13

A few minutes later, Sara wriggled out of Theo's arms. She couldn't afford to go to pieces, not now. She needed to be strong for Jake.

'I'm fine,' she said. 'I'm just fine. I know we're going to find him.' She looked back down the road, the way they had come earlier. 'If they left him here when they abandoned the car, would he know which way he needed to go to get back to the hospital? Suppose he started walking and someone else picked him up? I wouldn't leave a child on his own on a road like this, not when it's getting dark.'

It wasn't fear that was getting to her now; it was sheer frustration. She could cope with problems when they were cut and dried, like losing her job and the flat, but this time she had no idea what the problem was. Her son was missing, but she had no idea where to look for him, and that was tearing her apart.

A police car rounded the bend and came towards them slowly, hazard lights flashing. Her heart skipped a beat. Perhaps they'd found Jake. The brightly coloured car pulled up in front of them and a policeman in uniform got out.

He had been recruited from another village and had no idea who Sara and Theo were. It took them a minute to convince him not to arrest them. He had been driving the police car slowly all the way, he told them, and there had been no sign of a child.

'If we both turn around and go back the way we came,' Theo told him, 'we'll have covered this road twice in both directions.'

The policeman agreed, and Sara got back in Theo's car. She had been keeping herself going by telling herself they would find him any minute, either sitting beside the road or walking along the verge. Now it was beginning to hit her that he might be out all night. At the back of her mind was the thought that not everyone who picked up a child from beside a road was necessarily a Good Samaritan. Jake could be in more danger now than when he was in the car.

They had travelled half the distance back to the hospital when Sara asked Theo to stop.

He pulled over straight away. 'Did you see something?'

'I'm not sure.' She opened her door and got out. There were no houses beside the road, but a hedge of small trees and bushes separated a field of cows from the traffic. She peered into the bush nearest to her, wishing she had dressed Jake in something bright instead of his navy-blue top and knee-length shorts. She had thought for a moment that she'd seen a flash of something pale, like a child's face; but now there was nothing but the bushes, the darkening sky, and the misty shapes of grazing cows. They looked too big to be harmless, but she couldn't allow her fear to get in the way of finding Jake.

Rosie jumped out through the open door and ran off into the line of trees. Theo called to her, but she took no notice. 'She's probably seen a squirrel or a rat. She won't go after the cows.'

The little dog started barking, and he went after her while Sara called her son's name without much hope. There was little daylight left, and she could hardly make Theo out as he pushed his way into the field after his dog.

Sara could hear Rosie barking frantically, and then Theo appeared again, climbing up the bank with something in his arms.

'Jake?' She hardly dared let herself hope, but Theo put him down and he ran to her. She picked him up and he wrapped his legs round her waist, burying his head under her chin. She looked at Theo, feeling the tears running down her face.

'Where did you find him?'

Jake lifted his head and looked at her. 'Don't cry, Mummy, I was only hiding. I wanted to see the puppies, but I got put in their car and they took me away and then they told me to get out. I thought they might come back to get me. So I hid.'

She kissed her son, hugging him so tight he wriggled in her arms. 'They've gone. They won't ever come back, so you're safe now. And you've been very brave.'

'And very clever,' Theo added. 'It was clever of you to hide when you heard a car. Rosie found him,' he said to Sara. 'He might not have come out for me. He couldn't see who I was in the dark.'

Jake slid out of her arms to pet Rosie. 'She's clever too, isn't she, Theo? She knew where I was hiding.'

Theo took out his phone to report Jake's discovery to the police while Sara settled the boy in his booster seat and sat beside him, ready for the short ride back to the hospital. She never wanted to go through anything like that again, and she knew she would never forgive Milton Cassidy for causing her so much heartache. She still couldn't understand why the man seemed to want to punish her. She would have agreed to Jake seeing his grandfather on a regular basis if he had been even halfway reasonable. But now he would never set eyes on Jake again, she would make sure of that.

Aunt Marjory had already been told that Jake had been found safe and well. She was sitting inside the reception area of the hospital, another walking aid by her side. She got to her feet to hug Sara and then nearly crushed the life out of Jake. Rosie barked at her, and she put the little boy down.

'Rosie found Jake,' Sara told her. 'Jake was hiding because he was scared, and we might have driven on if it hadn't been for Rosie.'

'I wasn't scared,' Jake said indignantly. 'I was just being clever, like Theo said.'

Aunt Marjory said goodbye to the hospital staff and Theo helped her into the car. He folded her walker and fitted it in the back, helping Marjory into the front seat beside him. Rosie settled on the floor in the back with Sara and Jake.

Sara felt more tired than she ever had in her life before. Theo looked at her in his rear-view mirror as they drove out of the hospital gates. He smiled at her before he turned his eyes back to the road, and she managed to smile back at him. She had found her son, but she was about to lose the man she had come to depend on. She hoped he would leave as soon as possible. She would miss him dreadfully, but if he stayed any longer she would fall in love with him; and then, when he left, it would break her heart.

Aunt Marjory wanted to fuss. She had cake, she told Jake, and ice cream if he wanted some. There was also cold ham with fried eggs and chips, and she decided to open a can of baked beans. None of it took very long to prepare. Sara and Theo set the table while the oven chips were cooking.

'Why did those men take Jake?' Marjory asked once they were seated. She looked at Sara. 'You said something about Jake's grandfather. Why would he want to hurt his grandson? I don't understand.'

'I can't say much while we're eating.' Sara nodded her head towards Jake, hoping her aunt would realise she couldn't say much in front of her son. 'I'll try and explain some of it later. I owe you an explanation, but I don't understand the reason behind all this myself. It didn't serve any useful purpose, as far as I can see.'

They had almost finished their meal when her aunt's phone rang. She listened for a moment and then passed the phone to Theo.

'It's the police. They want to talk to you. They've caught the two men who abducted Jake.'

Theo took the phone and walked

outside into the hall; presumably, Sara thought, so Jake couldn't hear what he was saying. When he came back into the room, he shook his head. 'We'll talk later.'

All the secrecy was beginning to annoy Sara. What on earth had the police said that Jake shouldn't be allowed to hear? He would be pleased the men had been caught and presumably would soon be locked up. It would make him feel safe.

She told Jake he had fifteen minutes to finish his ice cream and then it would be a quick bath and bed. 'You'll still be here in the morning, won't you, Theo?' She tried to make her voice noncommittal, so it didn't sound as if she was trying to get him to stay. She kept telling herself she wanted him to go; Theo belonged in the city. He would never get used to country life. Sara hoped she would, because she had to. Perhaps she could rent a house near the main road where there was the sound of traffic, a long-distance lorry rumbling past in the early hours of the morning or the sound of a train in the distance. Anything but the thick silence that lay outside the windows of the bungalow, a silence that made her feel as if she was the only person left alive.

Jake was so tired he almost fell asleep in the bath. She had heard that children should have counselling after trauma, but at the moment Jake didn't seem particularly traumatised, so she thought she would play it by ear. If he needed help later on, she would make sure he got it.

She tucked him in and kissed him goodnight. She really wanted to lie down beside her child and watch him all night. She didn't want to let him out of her sight, not ever again. But being overprotective wouldn't do either of them any good, so she kissed him goodnight the way she always did, and joined Theo and her aunt in the living room.

Aunt Marjory had made coffee, and now she put a cafetière on the coffee table, together with three china mugs. Sara sat on the sofa beside Theo and poured coffee for all three of them.

'What did the police tell you that you couldn't mention in front of Jake?' She had wondered, while she was putting her son to bed, if the men had been overcome by fumes, or hit by another car.

'They found the men about half an hour ago.' He looked at Sara. 'One of the men was Spender, but he was the passenger. The car belonged to the other man. They were walking along the main Norwich road trying to hitch a lift, but it seems no one would pick them up in the dark.'

Aunt Marjory snorted. 'I don't blame anyone for leaving those two on the road. I would imagine they looked quite an undesirable pair, and it would have been fully dark by then.'

Sara frowned. 'Milton Cassidy must have hired Spender and that other man. Even if Spender organised the kidnapping, Cassidy was responsible.'

Theo shook his head. 'I don't think he was responsible for any of it, Sara, except sending you a solicitor's letter in the first place. I don't believe he had anything to do with Spender, or the other man in the car. In the end it was all about me, and I should have realised that.' He looked at Sara apologetically. 'I remembered why the driver of the car looked familiar, and then it all came together.'

'Sorry?' Sara had no idea what he was talking about. 'Of course Jake's grandfather is responsible. He chased us halfway across the country. I saw him on the road to Norwich.'

'I think you were mistaken, Sara. I said so at the time. There must be quite a few black chauffeur-driven saloon cars around.'

'Are you sure, Theo?' Aunt Marjory frowned. 'I've never seen one.'

Theo shrugged impatiently. 'The man I thought I recognised was Roger Kingsley's brother. He sent me a message saying, 'Now you know what it's like to lose someone you love.' He was talking about Jake, Sara.'

She was feeling completely bewildered. 'I still don't understand. You don't love Jake.'

He gave another irritable shrug. 'Of course I do, but that's beside the point. I'd seen Kingsley's brother in court. I phoned my sister while you were putting Jake to bed. He turned up at her house a couple of weeks ago looking for me, and she told him I'd gone away to recuperate. It wasn't Milton Cassidy looking for you, Sara; it was Roger Kingsley using his brother to look for me.'

Sara stared at him, glad she was already sitting down, because if she had been standing her legs might have given way. It was almost too much to take in all in one go. 'How long have you known?'

'Since yesterday. Up until then I wasn't sure, so I checked the family online and found a photo of Kingsley's brother. I'm sorry I didn't go to the police sooner, but I wanted to make sure I was right.'

'If you'd told the police yesterday, the men would have been arrested. They wouldn't have been around to kidnap Jake.' She turned away, unable to look at him any longer as the pieces dropped into place. 'It was nothing to do with us, was it? It was all to do with you. I've been hiding Jake for no reason. He was taken by those two men because of you. You waited before you said anything because you were afraid you might be wrong — and you're not used to being wrong, are you Theo? Everything that happened to me was because of you.'

'Not all of it.' He was sounding defensive now. 'You'd lost your job and your flat before you met me, that had nothing to do with me.'

'You don't understand, do you, Theo?' she said bitterly. 'I could cope with all of that. I've been through worse. But just when I thought we were safe, Spender turned up, and I was scared all over again. I thought Milton

Cassidy was determined to take Jake away from me. I thought he was going to use some fancy lawyer like you to prove I wasn't fit to look after my son. But when you said you wouldn't let that happen, I trusted you.'

'You can still trust me. The men have been arrested, and if Cassidy isn't involved, there's no one left to hurt Jake. You're both safe now.'

She shook her head. There was a sick feeling in the pit of her stomach that wouldn't go away. 'Apart from my father, I've only ever trusted two men, and they both let me down. Goodnight, Aunty. I'm going to bed. Perhaps I'll feel better in the morning.'

* * *

Theo watched Sara leave the room and then looked at her aunt. 'Do you think she will?'

Marjory stood up and made her way round the furniture to the other side of the room. 'Feel better? She might, but

266

she still won't forgive you. From the look on her face, she's going to need a bit longer than eight hours to do that.

Theo sighed. 'It wasn't all my fault.'

Marjory turned and looked at him, a frown bringing her eyebrows together. 'Now you sound like a petulant child. I would expect more backbone from a criminal lawyer.' She took a bottle out of a cupboard. 'I think we need something stronger than coffee, don't you? I have no idea what went on while I was in hospital, so you can fill me in, and then I might help you get Sara back on your side.' She waved a hand at him when he was about to speak. 'But that's only if I think you're worth it after I hear your side of the story.'

'Fair enough.' He took the bottle of Jack Daniels from her and filled a couple of shot glasses. 'It's a long story, so one of these might not be enough.'

Marjory settled back on her chair and lifted her injured foot onto the coffee table. 'First of all, why does someone want to hurt you, Theo?'

Theo explained about the shooting on the courtroom steps. 'Roger Kingsley is in prison and still has a couple of years to go; I checked. But his brother Derek threatened me after Roger got convicted of attempted murder. Derek Kingsley got taken out of court because of his foul language. He said his niece had been murdered and now I'd taken away his brother as well. He hired Spender to find me, and because of Spender's report, he thought Sara and Jake were important to me. Kidnapping Jake must have seemed like a good idea at the time.'

Marjory looked at him shrewdly. 'Are Sara and Jake important to you?'

He didn't hesitate. 'Yes, they are. Very important.'

'Good. She needs someone to look after her. She's been managing on her own for long enough.'

'She needs someone she can trust,' Theo said bitterly. 'And I don't fit the bill anymore.

Marjory leant across the table and

refilled their glasses. 'Tell me where Jake's grandfather fits in.'

Theo explained that Cassidy hadn't known he had a grandson until his son died. 'Dominic was an only child, and Cassidy had expected him to take over the family empire. He was devastated when his son died at such an early age. And then Sara sent a sympathy card saying she was a friend. Cassidy immediately checked up on her and found she'd been more than a friend. It didn't take him long to find out he had a grandson.'

Aunt Marjory looked round her comfortable sitting room. 'Sara doesn't belong here. She believes she can settle down out here in the country because it will be better for Jake, but a child can be happy anywhere as long as he's loved. The little boy had friends in London, didn't he?'

Theo nodded. 'He had three years at a nursery school near Sara's flat and would have been moving on to big school with children he already knows.'

'How about you?'

'Me?' Theo looked at Sara's aunt with a puzzled expression on his face. He wasn't sure what she was getting at.

'Yes, you. What are your long-term plans? You say you care about Sara and Jake, but where do they fit in? Do you want to make them both a part of your life, or do you want to leave them here, where you know they'll be safe, and go back to London on your own?'

Theo realised he had no idea what was going to happen next in his life. Could he go back to London without Sara and carry on where he left off? He didn't think he could. In fact, he was pretty damn sure he would be miserable without her.

'I was going to go back to London as soon as Sara got here, but then she found out you were in hospital, and we still thought Cassidy was trying to gather evidence against her.'

'That doesn't answer my question, Theo. If you want to leave here without Sara and Jake, there's nothing stopping

270

you. But I would suggest you go now, before either of them wake up. It will be easier that way.'

Theo finished his drink in one gulp. 'You know I can't do that.'

Marjory looked him straight in the eye, daring him to look away. 'I don't know any such thing. There's nothing stopping you walking out that door, driving back to your penthouse apartment in London, and getting on with your life. Why can't you do that?'

He took a deep breath. He wanted to look away, but Marjory's astute brown eyes refused to let him. 'You know why I can't.'

'You'll have to spell it out, Theo. I'm not going to play guessing games with you. Why can't you leave?'

'Dammit, Marjory! Because I can't imagine my life without Sara or Jake. We've sort of become a family, and I like being part of that.' He looked at the woman sitting opposite him and knew she wanted more. 'I think I'm falling in love with her, but I don't know how she feels, and we need to get to know one another in different circumstances.' He smiled. 'Ordinary circumstances. I'd like to take Sara out on a date, and take Jake to a football match — do ordinary things. This week has been crazy. We need to find out how well we get on in normal surroundings.'

'Do you think Sara really wants to stay here, or do you think she would prefer to go back to city life?'

'I think she'd love to go back to her life in London, but she can't afford it; and even if I offered to pay the rent on a flat, she wouldn't take money from me — or you.' He took a breath. 'And she certainly wouldn't agree to live with me, not yet.'

Marjory was silent for several minutes. 'Go to bed, Theo. Tell Sara I've asked you to stay until tomorrow evening.'

'It's no good talking to her,' Theo said tiredly. 'She won't listen to you.'

'I'm not going to talk to her, I'm going to try and sort out the mess you've managed to get yourselves into.'

Theo got to his feet. 'What are you going to do?' he asked worriedly.

Aunt Marjory smiled at him. 'I'm going to make a phone call,' she said.

14

Sara didn't sleep well. When she eventually felt it was late enough to start moving around, she had a quick look outside to make sure Theo's bedroom door was shut. She stood in the dimly lit hallway and listened outside his door. There was no sound from inside, and she wondered if he had already left. One part of her hoped he had. A quick, clean break was best for Jake. But the other part of her would be devastated. She felt she was owed at least a goodbye.

She left Jake asleep while she showered, and he was still soundly asleep when she began to dress. Something reasonably smart, she decided. Today would be the start of her hunt for rented accommodation, and she wanted to have a look at the nearby schools. She had hoped to get Jake accepted at the village school, but Aunt Marjory had said priority was given to local children, which was fair enough.

She brushed her hair and put on a slick of lip gloss in the light of the bedside lamp. When she pulled back the curtains, she would be able to see whether Theo's car was still parked in the driveway, and she was putting that moment off for as long as possible. She was muttering to herself about how stupid she was being, when Jake sat up in bed.

'Is it morning?'

'Yes.'

'Is it sunny?'

'Yes.' The sun had been coming up over the fields when she went to the bathroom.

'Can I go in the garden and play with Rosie until breakfast is ready?'

She wished she could just answer yes again. 'If Theo is still here. He may have had to leave early.'

Jake wriggled off the bed and shoved his feet into his slippers. 'But Rosie will still be here. She's staying with us, isn't she?'

It was obviously a rhetorical question, because Jake had grabbed his dressing gown and left the room, leaving the bedroom door wide open.

Sara was already dressed, so she went after him, but by the time she reached the end of the corridor she could hear Jake talking to someone in the kitchen. A few moments later she heard Rosie bark.

Theo looked up as she walked in the door. His hair was still tousled from the shower, and his bare feet had left damp marks on the kitchen tiles. 'Good morning,' he said a little warily.

She couldn't look at him and still be angry with him. She remembered the look on his face when he had carried Jake back to her. 'I'm sorry about last night,' she said. 'For having a go at you. I was tired and still a bit freaked out.'

'I'm not surprised. By the end of the day we were all a bit freaked out.'

Jake was dancing round the kitchen with Rosie chasing the cord of his dressing gown. Sara grabbed him by one arm. 'Shower, teeth and dress — in that order, young man, or there will be no breakfast for you.'

'I'll put coffee on,' Theo said.

'Give me ten minutes.' As she walked down the hall, Aunt Marjory was coming out of her room. 'Theo has coffee on,' Sara told her.

Aunt Marjory raised an eyebrow. 'So you're still talking to him?'

Jake said hello and then ran into the bathroom and shut the door. 'I've got to get to him before he turns on the shower,' Sara said. 'He'll get under the water with his dressing gown and slippers on if I don't stop him.' Which wasn't strictly true, but it gave her an excuse not to answer the question.

It took her longer than ten minutes, because Jake wanted to dress himself and couldn't get his socks on his still-damp feet, but she stalled a bit deliberately. She felt stupid for taking her tiredness out on Theo. He had done everything he could to help her from the first day she had met him. Part of the problem was that she didn't want him to go, but she couldn't ask him to stay. His whole life was centred in London, and hers wasn't — not anymore. If he wanted to see her after he left, he knew where to find her.

Theo and Aunt Marjory were sitting at the kitchen table drinking coffee. They had been talking about something, but stopped when Sara walked into the room. Theo handed her a mug of coffee and she set about getting Jake his toast and jam. It was probably not the healthiest breakfast in the world, but it was something he enjoyed, and that must count for something. She had tried to get him interested in cereal, but without much success. He didn't like the chocolate ones because they turned the milk a funny colour. Toast he loved, so she gave him wholemeal bread and expensive jam and a piece of fruit when she had it.

Theo had scrambled eggs and Sara piled some on a piece of toast for herself. She wondered if he cooked scrambled eggs for himself in his waterside apartment, or if he had someone to do it for him. Then she wondered why she was torturing herself. The big, beautiful man sitting in front of her didn't belong to her and never would, so she had to let him go and then try and forget about him.

'I promised Jake we'd take Rosie for a walk after breakfast,' Theo said. 'If you come too, maybe we could walk past the local school. Marjory says it's not too far from here. A ten-minute walk at most. I need to talk to you.'

'OK,' she said, slightly puzzled. She couldn't imagine what he wanted to talk to her about. They'd both already said everything they had to say, but a look at the school was a good idea. It would give her the chance to consider whether Jake would be happy there. She had discussed the school business with Jake and he had seemed quite philosophical about the whole thing, but she had a horrible feeling all that might change when he realised his friends weren't there with him and he didn't know any of the other children.

The sun was warm, so she put a light jacket on Jake and let him wear his sandals. Rosie was her usual boisterous self, and Theo's limp seemed nearly gone. The daffodils were going over, but gardens were full of tulips, hyacinths and crocuses, with magnolia flowers just about to open. At any other time it would have been a lovely way to spend a morning, but Theo was on edge about something, and that was making Sara nervous as well.

They found the school and watched as the children went into the playground, the little ones holding their parents' hands. In a few months' time, she would be taking Jake into a playground for the first time. The thought scared her, but she pushed it to one side. She had to make a new life for herself as well as her son.

Next to the school was a small play area with a few swings and a slide. Theo put Rosie on her lead and Jake ran off to try out the slide.

'What do you want to talk to me about?' she asked Theo. 'I know you've got to leave, and I really don't want to go over that again.' She turned her head to look at him and was surprised to see he appeared really worried. 'We can manage on our own, Theo. You don't have to worry about us. We'll be fine.'

'I know you will,' he said. 'And that's what's worrying me. I don't want you to be happy without me. I want you to miss me so much you'll slip into a decline like one of those Regency heroines.' He took her hand and smiled when she didn't pull it away. 'I want to carry on seeing you, Sara. I want to take you out on a date and get to know you. I want to be with you when you take Jake to school and watch him play in his first football match.'

She didn't know why he was doing this, why he was making it so hard for both of them. She had almost come to terms with never seeing him again, and a long-distance relationship wouldn't work. Jake needed someone who could do all the things Theo had been talking about, like going to football matches and parents' evenings. She wouldn't settle for him only seeing Theo occasionally at the weekend; they both needed more than that. And if that was all he could offer, she would rather be on her own.

'It won't work, Theo. I can't afford to move back to somewhere like Finsbury. My landlord wanted to get me out because then he could double the rent. I haven't even got a job anymore. If I get a job here, I can manage the rent on a flat or even a little house.' She took a breath. Even talking about going back to London upset her. 'Besides, it will be better for Jake to grow up in the country.'

'Who says? All Jake's friends are back in London. So are yours. I know he'll make new friends, because all kids do; but how about you, Sara?'

'I'll be fine.' She *had* been fine, until Theo started reminding her how much she missed everything she had left behind. She wanted to go out on a date with him, too, but not now and again when he could manage to get away. She wanted him to text her and suggest dinner and a show. Or bring a bottle round for a night in.

She stood up and called to Jake. 'We have to go. The school is nice, isn't it?' she asked as he ran back to her.

'Will Jason be there? He said we were both going to the same school.'

'I'm not sure,' she said, taking the cowardly way out. Why upset him now? By the time September came, she hoped he would have made some new friends.

They walked slowly back to the bungalow to find Aunt Marjory flapping a fluffy duster around. 'I don't know where it all comes from,' she said as they walked in the door.

Sara slipped off her jacket and took the duster from her aunt. 'You shouldn't be doing this. You're supposed to be resting.'

'You can probably blame Rosie for some of it,' Theo said. 'She hardly has any coat to speak of, but she still sheds a lot of hair.'

'Can I take her outside in the garden, Theo?' Jake asked eagerly. 'Then she won't make a mess in here.' When they all said yes at once, Jake called to Rosie and they both disappeared into the garden.

Sara looked at Theo, who was wandering around the room like a lost soul. 'Why don't you make some more coffee?' she suggested. If he didn't have anything to do, he might leave early so she'd do her best to keep him busy. She was beginning to regret her decision to cut him out of her life. As it got nearer the time for him to leave, even the odd weekend with him seemed like a good idea.

As she flicked the duster over already spotless surfaces, she looked out at Jake and Rosie playing in the garden. As soon as they had somewhere to live, she would get a dog. That might help make up for dragging Jake away from all his friends.

'I'm going to make some cakes,' Marjory said. 'Does Jake like jam tarts?'

'I do,' Theo called out from the kitchen.

'There's loads of jam, and I've got some frozen pastry in the freezer. It will thaw out while we have our coffee.'

'Did you make the jam?' Sara asked. She wondered if she would ever get to the stage where she made jam. She rather hoped that would never happen. She might finish up knitting, or doing something equally horrendous.

'Goodness me, no,' Marjory said. 'Beryl next door makes enough jam for the whole village.'

Sara noticed that her aunt kept looking out of the window; and what with the dusting and cake making, she wondered if Marjory was expecting a visitor. She was about to ask, but at that moment Theo walked in with a cafetière of coffee and she forgot all about it. She was beginning to realise that he only had to walk into the room for her to lose her train of thought. It was impossible, she told herself, to fall in love with a man after only a few days. Not only impossible, but irresponsible and foolhardy, and a lot more adjectives she would no doubt think of later.

Jake came in from the garden to tell her he was hungry, and that was always a bad omen. He could be quite objectionable when he was hungry. Theo offered to set the table while her aunt got on with making her jam tarts. Sara found a store-bought quiche in the fridge and put some tiny new potatoes on to boil. She had to wash them first to get rid of the soil and wondered if the lady next door had grown those as well.

They had finished eating, and Jake had gone back outside with Rosie, when a large car pulled up outside. Sara glanced out of the window and caught her breath. She had been right about

Cassidy passing them on the road, because now he was right outside her aunt's front door. Theo saw the look on her face and came round to stand beside her. He looked out of the window and then put his hand on her shoulder.

'He can't hurt you, Sara. I won't let him.'

'I'm sorry, I should have warned you,' Marjory said.

'How did he find us?' Sara felt numb. She had begun to think it was all over, that they could stop running, but now Milton Cassidy was standing outside and her aunt was going to let him in.

'I phoned him last night and told him you were here,' Marjory said. 'We had a long talk.' She looked at Sara pleadingly. 'He knows he made a mistake letting his lawyer send you that letter, but he is still Jake's grandfather. He's family, Sara.'

She shook her head vehemently. 'No!' she said. 'He's not any part of my family. I won't talk to him.'

'I never took you for a coward, Sara,' Theo said quietly. He squeezed her shoulder. 'What can he do to you?'

She had no idea, but she was sure it would be something diabolical. In her nightmares Cassidy had horns and breathed fire. He could do anything he liked. But then Theo moved his hand to her waist and pulled her towards him, and she felt the warmth of his body against hers.

'He's only a man, Sara, and you're not alone this time.'

Aunt Marjory opened the front door and let Milton Cassidy in, and Sara realised he *was* only a man. He had white hair and a walking stick, and he was a lot older than she had expected, but he held himself upright and looked at her with eyes that reminded her of Dominic.

Marjory asked him to sit down, and he lowered himself carefully into the armchair. Rosie walked over, wagging her tail, and Cassidy scratched her behind her ears. He was obviously used to dogs. Theo took the walking stick and propped it against the wall.

'An old injury,' Cassidy explained. 'I used to race cars.' He looked round the room. 'Where's the boy?'

'If you mean my son,' Sara said, trying to keep her voice steady, 'he's in the garden. I won't stop you seeing him, but I need to know why you're here.'

'After your reaction to my letter,' he said with a rueful smile, 'which I quite understand, I tried to trace you so I could speak to you personally, but I lost track of you when you left London.'

'I thought I saw you on the Norwich road.'

'You may have done. I found out your aunt was your only living relative and thought she might know how I could find you. I was tired after the journey, so I booked into a hotel in Norwich.'

'I phoned Milton last night,' Marjory said, 'and found he was in a hotel about a mile away. I explained about

Kevin Spender and the men who took Jake.'

Sara moved Theo's arm from around her waist. This was her problem, and she could handle it on her own, but it was nice to know he was there if she needed him. 'You wanted me to give you custody of my son, so you offered me — your words — a roof over my head and a better environment for my child. I don't need your money or your help, Mr Cassidy; and if that sounds ungrateful, I'm sorry.'

Marjory gave Sara a pleading look. 'May I offer you a cup of tea, Mr Cassidy?'

Sara nodded. There was no harm in being polite. 'I'll fetch Jake,' she said.

She made her way outside, wondering how she would explain the sudden appearance of a new family member. Up until that moment, Jake hadn't known he had a grandfather. She told him Cassidy was his father's daddy. 'He's come a long way just to see you, so go inside and say hello.' She'd done her best, but she had a bad feeling Jake wouldn't be content with that.

'Do you know my mummy?' he asked, standing in front of his grandfather.

'No, not really,' Cassidy said. 'But I'd like to get to know her, and you, Jake. That's why I came here, so I could get to know you both.'

'Did you know my daddy, too?'

'Yes, I did. I was his daddy.'

'That's enough questions,' Sara said before he could get out another one. 'Aunty Marjory has jam tarts in the kitchen. Go and help her bring them in, but be careful of the hot jam.'

'He's very bright for a four-year-old,' Cassidy said, 'and he seems happy and well adjusted. You're obviously bringing him up very well, and I apologise for suggesting otherwise.' He looked at Sara thoughtfully. 'I have a proposition for you, but it will depend on whether you want to stay here or go back to London.'

'I can't go back to London. The only reason I gave up our flat was because the landlord kept raising the rent. I don't get myself into debt, Mr Cassidy.'

'You took the same degree as Dominic, didn't you? Business studies.'

'We both took an MA in business management. That's how I first met your son.'

'I have a team of accountants for the business side of things, but Dominic had been handling everything else. I'm finding it difficult. The staff still have to be paid, and I own a few race horses. We also hold a jazz concert in the grounds once a year. Managing the accounts for all that is quite a big job, and I haven't yet found anyone to take Dominic's place.'

Sara wasn't sure what point he was trying to make. 'When I met Dominic, we were both very young. We had fun together and got on really well, but Dominic didn't want the responsibility of a child. I knew that. He told me right from the beginning he wasn't interested in a long-term relationship. Marriage, babies, that wasn't part of his plan.'

'So you never told him you were pregnant with his child.'

'We'd already split up. There was no need to tell him.'

She hadn't wanted to tie Dominic down or make him feel responsible for a child he didn't want. She had been sure she could manage on her own, and she had. She had been scared of being in exactly this position — beholden to the Cassidy family for the rest of her life. But now Milton was making her feel guilty.

'My grandson is all I have left now,' Milton said, 'and I would like him to have the same chance his father did. I want him to be able to go to university without having to worry about the cost.' He smiled at Marjory when she put a cup of tea and a plate of jam tarts in front of him. 'I came here to ask a favour, Sara. I don't want to put the financial affairs of my household in the hands of a stranger, so I'm asking if you'll take over Dominic's position.' He held up his hand when she started to protest. 'I have an office building on the banks of the Thames near a Tube station, and there's a generous living allowance included in the package. I'm sure you could afford to rent one of those little Victorian houses in Finsbury Park near Jake's friends.'

Sara wanted to say no. She had spent weeks refusing to have anything to do with this man. She considered him arrogant in the worst possible way, but — and this was a big but — if she said no, was she just being obstinate and selfish? Probably.

'I'd love to go back to London. The longer I stay here, the more I realise I'm not a country girl. I'm still afraid of cows.' She took a breath. 'And I know I could do the job you're offering me, but I'd be beholden to you forever, wouldn't I, Mr Cassidy? You'd always want complete control.'

Cassidy shrugged. 'I want to be able to see my grandson on a regular basis, Sara, but I have no wish to take over your life.'

Theo put his arm round her again, and Jake looked at her expectantly. He might not be sure what was going on, but he had heard his name mentioned. Sara looked round the room and realised everyone was waiting for her to make a decision.

'How would you like to go back to London to live so you start big school with your friends?' Maybe she was being unfair, even cowardly, to leave one of the biggest decisions of their lives up to a four-year-old, but it was his choice as much as hers.

Jake looked up at Theo. 'Will I still be able to play with Rosie?'

'She doesn't live with me, Jake, because she belongs to my sister, but you can play with her at my sister's house. My sister has a little boy you can play with as well.'

'And you can all come here and visit me in the summer,' Aunt Marjory said. 'Perhaps you can bring Rosie with you.'

Theo's arm tightened round Sara's waist. 'And if we're both working in

London, I can meet you after work and take you on a date. We can begin the business of getting to know one another.'

Aunt Marjory breathed a sigh of relief. 'That's settled then.'

Sara looked across the room at the man who could possibly have been her father-in-law. 'It looks as if I'm going to accept your offer, Milton, so thank you.'

15

The car was white, and it had ribbons tied to the front. But it wasn't a big limousine, it was a Mini, and her best friend was driving. Lettie got out of the car when she saw Sara coming towards her.

'Wow! You look amazing. I was a bit disappointed when you told me you weren't getting married in a big white dress, but you did the right thing, girl. There's nothing disappointing about that dress.'

Sara did a little twirl. 'You think?'

The look of admiration on Lettie's face had taken away any doubts Sara might have had. She had spent nearly a month looking for exactly the right thing. Not too flamboyant, but not too safe, either. The dress she had eventually chosen was a little wisp of creamy lace over a shift of pink satin. The neckline was quite modest, but the scalloped hem stopped several inches above her knees. She had good legs, so why not exploit them. No hat — she hated hats — but she had flowers in her hair and cream sandals with spiked heels on her bare feet.

There was a crowd of people outside the little chapel; people who had stopped to watch when they realised a wedding was taking place; people who cheered when Sara got out of the car. Feeling like royalty, she stepped into the coolness inside, her eyes going to the top of the aisle to make sure Theo was already there.

He was standing with his back to her, with Jake, his best man, by his side. She could see the tension in his shoulders even at a distance, and she smiled to herself when she realised he had been wondering if she would turn up.

She felt someone take her arm, and smiled at Milton Cassidy as he moved his walking stick to his other hand. When she had asked if he would give her away, the look of astonished delight on his face had put everything in perspective. He had lost his only son, and allowing him the pleasure of a grandson was a small price to pay.

The music started, and Theo turned round to watch her walk towards him. He smiled and took Jake's hand in his. Aunt Marjory was right up the front, taking the place of Sara's mother, with Theo's sister and nephew at her side; and Sara spotted a couple of Jake's best friends from school, dressed in their best and already looking bored.

Milton stepped to one side and she took a big, happy breath. She had family now. In a few minutes she would have a husband, a son, and a proxy mother and father. Her friends were there to support her because she was back in London, and she was back in London because of Milton Cassidy. Fate really did work in mysterious ways.

She reached for Theo's hand and felt the slight tremble in his fingers. He would never show he was scared, but she had a feeling he was absolutely terrified. They had both decided not to make a speech about how much they adored each other; but after the formal part was over, Theo said 'I love you, Sara Winter' loudly enough for everyone to hear.

The service was short, and when they came out of the chapel Milton insisted he drive them to the reception. She had left the organising of the reception to Theo because he had wanted to get involved, but she had insisted it would be somewhere simple and not too many people would be invited. As she settled in the back of Milton's Bentley, with Theo on one side and Jake on the other, she had to admit there were times when a little luxury didn't go amiss.

As they left the centre of London, she turned to look at Theo. He was holding her hand, but he looked a little apprehensive, and she hoped he wasn't having second thoughts. As it was, he'd left it a bit late. She was now Mrs Sara

Winter, and as soon as they got back from their honeymoon, she would have Jake's name changed as well.

'Where are we going, Theo?'

He gave her hand a squeeze. 'After you eventually agreed to marry me, you wanted it all organised in a couple of weeks. It's not easy in London.'

'There are lots of bars and cafés that would have let us have a big table. I told you I didn't want too many people, just family and a few friends.'

'That's all it's going to be, family and friends. But you may not like the venue.' Before she could answer, he looked out of the window. 'Anyway, it's too late to change it now. We're nearly there.'

His anxiety was beginning to affect her as well. What on earth had he done? 'Did you find somewhere for Aunt Marjory to spend the night?'

When he nodded, she turned her attention to the view outside the window, trying to work out where they were. The road they were in was wide with enormous grass verges, and most of the houses were set back behind either a high wall or hedge. When the car stopped in front of a pair of wrought-iron gates and they opened automatically, she turned in her seat to glare at Theo.

He was doing his best to look innocent. 'Milton wanted to help in some way, and I was having trouble booking anywhere. It's only a tent in his back garden, Sara. Nothing posh.'

When she saw the marquee, she decided to give in gracefully. It was quite small, as marquees go, but she had never seen anything quite so beautiful. The inside was decorated with satin ribbon streamers and bows, while mobiles of brightly coloured butterflies hung from the high roof. She had never seen so many flowers all in one place. The finger food was served on a long buffet table or carried around by waiters with silver trays, the champagne was unlimited and arrived in tall crystal glasses, and Milton had made sure there were plenty of non-alcoholic drinks for the children or anyone driving home. He had provided a few tables and small gilt chairs for the older people, but everyone seemed happy to stand around and mingle.

Theo had left her to circulate among the guests, and when he found her again she had a glass of champagne in one hand and a tiny caviar and smoked salmon vol-au-vent in the other.

'Do I get to kiss my wife?'

She shook her head. 'Not when I've been eating fish.' She looked at him hopefully. 'This is wonderful, Theo, but can we go now?'

'I'm glad you're not cross with me about coming here for the reception. Milton is looking after Aunt Marjory and a couple of other people and will put them up for the night. He really has been helpful.' He looked her up and down. 'You look absolutely wonderful, Sara. I can't believe you're all mine.'

'I'm not,' she said. 'Maybe you can have half of me to start with.'

'Which half?' he asked innocently.

'You'll have to wait and see.' She looked round at her guests. They all appeared to be enjoying themselves. 'I need to say goodbye to everyone.'

'Do you need to change before we leave?'

She shook her head. She had got her own way with the honeymoon. Jake only had two more weeks before he started at his new school, and Sara felt she owed him a proper holiday, so they were taking him with them to a country-house hotel on the Sussex coast. It was all-inclusive, welcomed children, and was on a beautiful stretch of sandy beach. When they got back, they would all move into their new house. The exotic holidays would keep for later. They had the rest of their lives to see the world.

Milton's chauffeur was driving them to their hotel, so she made sure the cases were in the back, and then went round saying goodbye to everyone. She found Milton in the summerhouse, which was bigger than her previous flat, pouring brandy from a cut-glass decanter.

When he saw Sara, he raised his glass. 'Congratulations, Mrs Winter. I hope you enjoyed the reception. I have a villa in the Caribbean, you know. You could have gone there for your honeymoon.'

'No, we couldn't, Milton. I told you right at the beginning, I won't ever let you have complete control. But I do appreciate a little help now and again, so thank you for all you've done.'

He smiled at her. 'Enjoy your holiday, Sara. Come and see me when you get back.'

'We will,' she promised. 'Jake will want to show you his new puppy.'

All in all, she thought, once the storm was over it had all worked out rather well.

We do hope that you have enjoyed reading this large print book.

Did you know that all of our titles are available for purchase?

We publish a wide range of high quality large print books including:
Romances, Mysteries, Classics General Fiction Non Fiction and Westerns

Special interest titles available in large print are:
The Little Oxford Dictionary Music Book, Song Book Hymn Book, Service Book

Also available from us courtesy of Oxford University Press:
Young Readers' Dictionary (large print edition) Young Readers' Thesaurus (large print edition)

For further information or a free brochure, please contact us at:
Ulverscroft Large Print Books Ltd., The Green, Bradgate Road, Anstey, Leicester, LE7 7FU, England. Tel: (00 44) 0116 236 4325 **Fax:** (00 44) 0116 234 0205